I0541060

The Three Eyes

Maurice Leblanc

The Three Eyes

Copyright © 2021 Bibliotech Press
All rights reserved

The present edition is a reproduction of previous publication of this classic work. Minor typographical errors may have been corrected without note; however, for an authentic reading experience the spelling, punctuation, and capitalization have been retained from the original text.

ISBN: 978-1-63637-745-2

CONTENTS

Chapter

I	Bergeronnette	1
II	The "Triangular Circles"	8
III	An Execution	16
IV	Noël Dorgeroux's Son	22
V	The Kiss	29
VI	Anxieties	38
VII	The Fierce-Eyed Man	45
VIII	"Some One Will Emerge from the Darkness"	52
IX	The Man Who Emerged From the Darkness	61
X	The Crowd Sees	69
XI	The Cathedral	75
XII	The "Shapes"	81
XIII	The Veil is Lifted	89
XIV	Massignac and Velmot	100
XV	The Splendid Theory	106
XVI	Where Lips Unite	117
XVII	Supreme Visions	124
XVIII	The Château de Pré-Bony	130
XIX	The Formula	139

CHAPTER I

BERGERONNETTE

For me the strange story dates back to that autumn day when my uncle Dorgeroux appeared, staggering and unhinged, in the doorway of the room which I occupied in his house, Haut-Meudon Lodge.

None of us had set eyes on him for a week. A prey to that nervous exasperation into which the final test of any of his inventions invariably threw him, he was living among his furnaces and retorts, keeping every door shut, sleeping on a sofa, eating nothing but fruit and bread. And suddenly he stood before me, livid, wild-eyed, stammering, emaciated, as though he had lately recovered from a long and dangerous illness.

He was really altered beyond recognition! For the first time I saw him wear unbuttoned the long, threadbare, stained frock-coat which fitted his figure closely and which he never discarded even when making his experiments or arranging on the shelves of his laboratories the innumerable chemicals which he was in the habit of employing. His white tie, which, by way of contrast, was always clean, had become unfastened; and his shirt-front was protruding from his waistcoat. As for his good, kind face, usually so grave and placid and still so young beneath the white curls that crowned his head, its features seemed unfamiliar, ravaged by conflicting expressions, no one of which obtained the upper hand over the others: violent expressions of terror and anguish in which I was surprised, at moments, to observe gleams of the maddest and most extravagant delight.

I could not get over my astonishment. What had happened during those few days? What tragedy could have caused the quiet, gentle Noël Dorgeroux to be so utterly beside himself?

"Are you ill, uncle?" I asked, anxiously, for I was exceedingly fond of him.

"No," he murmured, "no, I'm not ill."

"Then what is it? Please, what's the matter?"

"Nothing's the matter ... nothing, I tell you."

I drew up a chair. He dropped into it and, at my entreaty, took a glass of water; but his hand trembled so that he was unable to lift it to his lips.

"Uncle, speak, for goodness' sake!" I cried. "I have never seen you in such a state. You must have gone through some great excitement."

"The greatest excitement of my life," he said, in a very low and lifeless voice. "Such excitement as nobody can have ever experienced before ... nobody ... nobody...."

"Then do explain yourself."

"No, you wouldn't understand.... I don't understand either. It's so incredible! It is taking place in the darkness, in a world of darkness! ..."

There was a pencil and paper on the table. His hand seized the pencil; and mechanically he began to trace one of those vague sketches to which the action of an overmastering idea gradually imparts a clearer definition. And his sketch, as it assumed a more distinct form, ended by representing on the sheet of white paper three geometrical figures which might equally well have been badly-described circles or triangles with curved lines. In the centre of these figures, however, he drew a regular circle which he blackened entirely and which he marked in the middle with a still blacker point, as the iris is marked with the pupil:

"There, there!" he cried, suddenly, starting up in his agitation. "Look, that's what is throbbing and quivering in the darkness. Isn't it enough to drive one mad? Look! ..."

He had seized another pencil, a red one, and, rushing to the wall, he scored the white plaster with the same three incomprehensible figures, the three "triangular circles," in the centre of which he took the pains to draw irises furnished with pupils:

"Look! They're alive, aren't they? You see they're moving, you can see that they're afraid. You can see, can't you? They're alive! They're alive!"

I thought that he was going to explain. But, if so, he did not carry out his intention. His eyes, which were generally full of life, frank and open as a child's, now bore an expression of distrust. He began to walk up and down and continued to do so for a few minutes. Then, at last, opening the door and turning to me again, he said, in the same breathless tone as before:

"You will see them, Vivien; you will have to see them too and tell me that they are alive, as I have seen them alive. Come to the Yard in an hour's time, or rather when you hear a whistle, and you shall see them, the three eyes, and plenty of other things besides. You'll see."

He left the room.

The house in which we lived, the Lodge, as it was called, turned its back upon the street and faced an old, steep, ill-kept garden, at

2

the top of which was the big yard in which my uncle had now for many years been squandering the remnants of his capital on useless inventions.

As far back as I could remember, I had always seen that old garden ill-tended and the long, low house in a constant state of dilapidation, with its yellow plaster front cracked and peeling. I used to live there in the old days with my mother, who was my aunt Dorgeroux's sister. Afterwards, when both the sisters were dead, I used to come from Paris, where I was going through a course of study, to spend my holidays with my uncle. He was then mourning the death of his poor son Dominique, who was treacherously murdered by a German airman whom he had brought to the ground after a terrific fight in the clouds. My visits to some extent diverted my uncle's thoughts from his grief. But I had had to go abroad; and it was not until after a very long absence that I returned to Haut-Meudon Lodge, where I had now been some weeks, waiting for the end of the vacation and for my appointment as a professor at Grenoble.

And at each of my visits I had found the same habits, the same regular hours devoted to meals and walks, the same monotonous life, interrupted, at the time of the great experiments, by the same hopes and the same disappointments. It was a healthy, vigorous life, which suited the tastes and the extravagant dreams of Noël Dorgeroux, whose courage and confidence no trial was able to defeat or diminish.

I opened my window. The sun shone down upon the walls and buildings of the Yard. Not a cloud tempered the blazing sky. A scent of late roses quivered on the windless air.

"Victorien!" whispered a voice below me, from a hornbeam overgrown with red creeper.

I knew that it must be Bérangère, my uncle's god-daughter, reading, as usual, on a stone bench, her favourite seat.

"Have you seen your god-father?" I asked.

"Yes," she replied. "He was going through the garden and back to his Yard. He looked so queer!"

Bérangère pushed aside the leafy curtain at a place where the trelliswork which closed the arbour was broken; and her pretty face, crowned with rebellious golden curls, came into view.

"This is pleasant!" she said laughing. "My hair's caught. And there are spiders' webs too. Ugh! Help!"

These are childish recollections, insignificant details. Yet why did they remain engraved on my memory with such precision? It is as though all our being becomes charged with emotion at the approach of the great events which we are fated to encounter and our senses thrilled beforehand by the impalpable breath of a distant storm.

I hastened down the garden and ran to the hornbeam. Bérangère was gone. I called her. I received a merry laugh in reply and saw her farther away, swinging on a rope which she had stretched between two trees, under an arch of leaves.

She was delicious like that, graceful and light as a bird perched on some swaying bough. At each swoop, all her curls flew now in this direction, now in that, giving her a sort of moving halo, with which mingled the leaves that fell from the shaken trees, red leaves, yellow leaves, leaves of every shade of autumn gold.

Notwithstanding the anxiety with which my uncle's excessive agitation had filled my mind, I lingered before the sight of this incomparable light-heartedness and, giving the girl the pet name formed years ago from her Christian name of Bérangère, I said, under my voice and almost unconsciously:

"Bergeronnette!"

She jumped out of her swing and, planting herself in front of me, said:

"You're not to call me that any longer, Mr. Professor!"

"Why not?"

"It was all right once, when I was a little mischief of a tomboy, hopping and skipping all over the place. But now ..."

"Well, your god-father still calls you that."

"My god-father has every right to."

"And I?"

"No right at all."

This is not a love-story; and I did not mean to speak of Bérangère before coming to the momentous part which, as everybody knows, she played in the adventure of the Three Eyes. But this part was so closely interwoven, from the beginning and during all the early period of the adventure, with certain episodes of our intimate life that the clearness of my narrative would suffer if it were not mentioned, however briefly.

Well, twelve years before the time of which I am speaking, there arrived at the Lodge a little girl to whom my uncle was god-father and from whom he used to receive a letter regularly on each 1st of January, bringing him her good wishes for the new year. She lived at Toulouse with her father and mother, who had formerly been in business at Meudon, near my uncle's place. Now the mother had died; and the father, without further ceremony, sent the daughter to Noël Dorgeroux with a short letter of which I remember a few sentences:

4

"The child is dull here, in the town.... My business" — Massignac was a wine-agent—" takes me all over the country ... and Bérangère is left behind alone.... I was thinking that, in memory of our friendly relations, you might be willing to keep her with you for a few weeks.... The country air will restore the colour to her cheeks...."

My uncle was a very kindly, good-hearted man. The few weeks were followed by several months and then by several years, during which the worthy Massignac at intervals announced his intention of coming to Meudon to fetch the child. So it came about that Bérangère did not leave the Lodge at all and that she surrounded my uncle with so much gay and boisterous affection that, in spite of his apparent indifference, Noël Dorgeroux had felt unable to part with his god-daughter. She enlivened the silent old house with her laughter and her charm. She was the element of disorder and delightful irresponsibility which gives a value to order, discipline and austerity.

Returning this year after a long absence, I had found, instead of the child whom I had known, a girl of twenty, just as much a child and just as boisterous as ever, but exquisitely pretty, graceful in form and movement and possessed of the mystery which marks those who have led solitary lives within the shadow of an old and habitually silent man. From the first I felt that my presence interfered with her habits of freedom and isolation. At once audacious and shy, timid and provocative, bold and shrinking, she seemed to shun me in particular; and, during two months of a life lived in common, when I saw her at every meal and met her at every turn, I had failed to tame her. She remained remote and wild, suddenly breaking off our talks and displaying, where I was concerned, the most capricious and inexplicable moods.

Perhaps she had an intuition of the profound disturbance that was awaking within me; perhaps her confusion was due to my own embarrassment. She had often caught my eyes fixed on her red lips or observed the change that came over my voice at certain times. And she did not like it. Man's admiration disconcerted her.

"Look here," I said, adopting a roundabout method so as not to startle her, "your god-father maintains that human beings, some of them more than others, give forth a kind of emanation. Remember that Noël Dorgeroux is first and foremost a chemist and that he sees and feels things from the chemist's point of view. Well, to his mind, this emanation is manifested by the emission of certain corpuscles, of invisible sparks which form a sort of cloud. This is what happens, for instance, in the case of a woman. Her charm surrounds you ..."

My heart was beating so violently as I spoke these words that I had to break off. Still, she did not seem to grasp their meaning; and she said, with a proud little air:

"Your uncle tells me all about his theories. It's true, I don't understand them a bit. However, as regards this one, he has spoken to me of a special ray, which he presupposed to explain that discharge of invisible particles. And he calls this ray after the first letter of my name, the B-ray."

"Well done, Bérangère; that makes you the god-mother of a ray, the ray of seductiveness and charm."

"Not at all," she cried, impatiently. "It's not a question of seductiveness but of a material incarnation, a fluid which is even able to become visible and to assume a form, like the apparitions produced by the mediums. For instance, the other day ..."

She stopped and hesitated; her face betrayed anxiety; and I had to press her before she continued:

"No, no," she said, "I oughtn't to speak of that. It's not that your uncle forbade me to. But it has left such a painful impression...."

"What do you mean, Bérangère?"

"I mean, an impression of fear and suffering. I saw, with your uncle, on a wall in the Yard, the most frightful things: images which represented three—sort of eyes. Were they eyes? I don't know. The things moved and looked at us. Oh, I shall never forget it as long as I live."

"And my uncle?"

"Your uncle was absolutely taken aback. I had to hold him up and bring him round, for he fainted. When he came to himself, the images had vanished."

"And did he say nothing?"

"He stood silent, gazing at the wall. Then I asked him, 'What is it, god-father?' Presently he answered, 'I don't know, I don't know: it may be the rays of which I spoke to you, the B-rays. If so, it must be a phenomenon of materialization.' That was all he said. Very soon after, he saw me to the door of the garden; and he has shut himself up in the Yard ever since. I did not see him again until just now."

She ceased. I felt anxious and greatly puzzled by this revelation:

"Then, according to you, Bérangère," I said, "my uncle's discovery is connected with those three figures? They were geometrical figures, weren't they? Triangles?"

She formed a triangle with her two fore-fingers and her two thumbs:

"There, the shape was like that.... As for their arrangement ..."

6

She picked up a twig that had fallen from a tree and was beginning to draw lines in the sand of the path when a whistle sounded.

"That's god-father's signal when he wants me in the Yard," she cried.

"No," I said, "to-day it's for me. We fixed it."

"Does he want you?"

"Yes, to tell me about his discovery."

"Then I'll come too."

"He doesn't expect you, Bérangère."

"Yes, he does; yes, he does."

I caught hold of her arm, but she escaped me and ran to the top of the garden, where I came up with her outside a small, massive door in a fence of thick planks which connected a shed and a very high wall.

She opened the door an inch or two. I insisted:

"Don't do it, Bérangère! It will only vex him."

"Do you really think so?" she said, wavering a little.

"I'm positive of it, because he asked me and no one else. Come, Bérangère, be sensible."

She hesitated. I went through and closed the door upon her.

CHAPTER II

THE "TRIANGULAR CIRCLES"

What was known at Meudon as Noël Dorgeroux's Yard was a piece of waste-land in which the paths were lost amid the withered grass, nettles and stones, amid stacks of empty barrels, scrap-iron, rabbit-hutches and every kind of disused lumber that rusts and rots or tumbles into dust.

Against the walls and outer fences stood the workshops, joined together by driving-belts and shafts, and the laboratories filled with furnaces, pneumatic receivers, innumerable retorts, phials and jars containing the most delicate products of organic chemistry.

The view embraced the loop of the Seine, which lay some three hundred feet below, and the hills of Versailles and Sèvres, which formed a wide circle on the horizon towards which a bright autumnal sun was sinking in a pale blue sky.

"Victorien!"

My uncle was beckoning to me from the doorway of the workshop which he used most often. I crossed the Yard.

"Come in," he said. "We must have a talk first. Only for a little while: just a few words."

The room was lofty and spacious and one corner of it was reserved for writing and resting, with a desk littered with papers and drawings, a couch and some old, upholstered easy-chairs. My uncle drew one of the chairs up for me. He seemed calmer, but his glance retained an unaccustomed brilliance.

"Yes," he said, "a few words of explanation beforehand will do no harm, a few words on the past, the wretched past which is that of every inventor who sees fortune slipping away from him. I have pursued it for so long! I have always pursued it. My brain had always seemed to me a vat in which a thousand incoherent ideas were fermenting, all contradicting one another and mutually destructive.... And then there was one that gained strength. And thenceforward I lived for that one only and sacrificed everything for it. It was like a sink that swallowed up all my money and that of others ... and their happiness and peace of mind as well. Think of my poor wife, Victorien. You remember how unhappy she was and how anxious about the future of her son, of my poor Dominique! And yet I loved her so devotedly...."

He stopped at this recollection. And I seemed to see my aunt's

8

face again and to hear her telling my mother of her fears and her forebodings:

"He will ruin us," she used to say. "He keeps on making me sell out. He considers nothing."

"She did not trust me," Noël Dorgeroux continued. "Oh, I had so many disappointments, so many lamentable failures! Do you remember, Victorien, do you remember my experiment on intensive germination by means of electric currents, my experiments with oxygen and all the rest, all the rest, not one of which succeeded? The pluck it called for! But I never lost faith for a minute! ... One idea in particular buoyed me up and I came back to it incessantly, as though I were able to penetrate the future. You know to what I refer, Victorien: it appeared and reappeared a score of times under different forms, but the principle remained the same. It was the idea of utilizing the solar heat. It's all there, you know, in the sun, in its action upon us, upon cells, organisms, atoms, upon all the more or less mysterious substances that nature has placed at our disposal. And I attacked the problem from every side. Plants, fertilizers, diseases of men and animals, photographs: for all these I wanted the collaboration of the solar rays, utilized by the aid of special processes which were mine alone, my secret and nobody else's."

My uncle Dorgeroux was talking with renewed eagerness; and his eyes shone feverishly. He now held forth without interrupting himself:

"I will not deny that there was an element of chance about my discovery. Chance plays its part in everything. There never was a discovery that did not exceed our inventive effort; and I can confess to you, Victorien, that I do not even now understand what has happened. No, I can't explain it by a long way; and I can only just believe it. But, all the same, if I had not sought in that direction, the thing would not have occurred. It was due to me that the incomprehensible miracle took place. The picture is outlined in the very frame which I constructed, on the very canvas which I prepared; and, as you will perceive, Victorien, it is my will that makes the phantom which you are about to see emerge from the darkness."

He expressed himself in a tone of pride with which was mingled a certain uneasiness, as though he doubted himself and as though his words overstepped the actual limits of truth.

"You're referring to those three—sort of eyes, aren't you?" I asked.

"What's that?" he exclaimed, with a start. "Who told you? Bérangère, I suppose! She shouldn't have. That's what we must avoid at all costs: indiscretions. One word too much and I am undone; my discovery is stolen. Only think, the first man that comes along ...”

I had risen from my chair. He pushed me towards his desk:

“Sit down here, Victorien,” he said, “and write. You mustn't mind my taking this precaution. It is essential. You must realize what you are pledging yourself to do if you share in my work. Write, Victorien.”

“What, uncle?”

“A declaration in which you acknowledge that ... But I'll dictate it to you. That'll be better.”

I interrupted him:

“Uncle, you distrust me.”

“I don't distrust you, my boy. I fear an imprudence, an indiscretion. And, generally speaking, I have plenty of reasons for being suspicious.”

“What reasons, uncle?”

“Reasons,” he replied, in a more serious voice, “which make me think that I am being spied upon and that somebody is trying to discover what my invention is. Yes, somebody came in here, the other night, and rummaged among my papers.”

“Did they find anything?”

“No. I always carry the most important notes and formulae on me. Still, you can imagine what would happen if they succeeded. So you do admit, don't you, that I am obliged to be cautious? Write down that I have told you of my investigations and that you have seen what I obtain on the wall in the Yard, at the place covered by a black-serge curtain.”

I took a sheet of paper and a pen. But he stopped me quickly:

“No, no,” he said, “it's absurd. It wouldn't prevent ... Besides, you won't talk, I'm sure of that. Forgive me, Victorien. I am so horribly worried!”

“You needn't fear any indiscretion on my part,” I declared. “But I must remind you that Bérangère also has seen what there was to see.”

“Oh,” he said, “she wouldn't understand!”

“She wanted to come with me just now.”

“On no account, on no account! She's still a child and not fit to be trusted with a secret of this importance.... Now come along.”

But it so happened that, as we were leaving the workshop, we both of us at the same time saw Bérangère stealing along one of the walls of the Yard and stopping in front of a black curtain, which she suddenly pulled aside.

“Bérangère!” shouted my uncle, angrily.

The girl turned round and laughed.

"I won't have it! I will not have it!" cried Noël Dorgeroux, rushing in her direction. "I won't have it, I tell you! Get out, you mischief!"

Bérangère ran away, without, however, displaying any great perturbation. She leapt on a stack of bricks, scrambled on to a long plank which formed a bridge between two barrels and began to dance as she was wont to do, with her arms outstretched like a balancing-pole and her bust thrown slightly backwards.

"You'll lose your balance," I said, while my uncle drew the curtain.

"Never!" she replied, jumping up and down on her spring-board.

She did not lose her balance. But the plank shifted and the pretty dancer came tumbling down among a heap of old packing-cases.

I ran to her assistance and found her lying on the ground, looking very white.

"Have you hurt yourself, Bérangère?"

"No ... hardly ... just my ankle ... perhaps I've sprained it."

I lifted her, almost fainting, in my arms and carried her to a wooden bench a little farther away.

She let me have my way and even put one arm round my neck. Her eyes were closed. Her red lips opened and I inhaled the cool fragrance of her breath.

"Bérangère!" I whispered, trembling with emotion.

When I laid her on the bench, her arm held me more tightly, so that I had to bend my head with my face almost touching hers. I meant to draw back. But the temptation was too much for me and I kissed her on the lips, gently at first and then with a brutal violence which brought her to her senses.

She repelled me with an indignant movement and stammered, in a despairing, rebellious tone:

"Oh, it's abominable of you! ... It's shameful!"

In spite of the suffering caused by her sprain, she had managed to stand up, while I, stupefied by my thoughtless conduct, stood bowed before her, without daring to raise my head.

We remained for some seconds in this attitude, in an embarrassed silence through which I could catch the hurried rhythm of her breathing. I tried gently to take her hands. But she released them at once and said:

"Let me be. I shall never forgive you, never."

"Come, Bérangère, you will forget that."

"Leave me alone. I want to go indoors."

"But you can't, Bérangère."

11

"Here's god-father. He'll take me back."

My reasons for relating this incident will appear in the sequel. For the moment, notwithstanding the profound commotion produced by the kiss which I had stolen from Bérangère, my thoughts were so to speak absorbed by the mysterious drama in which I was about to play a part with my uncle Dorgeroux. I heard my uncle asking Bérangère if she was not hurt. I saw her leaning on his arm and, with him, making for the door of the garden. But, while I remained bewildered, trembling, dazed by the adorable image of the girl whom I loved, it was my uncle whom I awaited and whom I was impatient to see returning. The great riddle already held me captive.

"Let's make haste," cried Noël Dorgeroux, when he came back. "Else it will be too late and we shall have to wait until to-morrow."

He led the way to the high wall where he had caught Bérangère in the act of yielding to her curiosity. This wall, which divided the Yard from the garden and which I had not remarked particularly on my rare visits to the Yard, was now daubed with a motley mixture of colours, like a painter's palette. Red ochre, indigo, purple and saffron were spread over it in thick and uneven layers, which whirled around a more thickly-coated centre. But, at the far end, a wide curtain of black serge, like a photographer's cloth, running on an iron rod supported by brackets, hid a rectangular space some three or four yards in width.

"What's that?" I asked my uncle. "Is this the place?"

"Yes," he answered, in a husky voice, "it's behind there."

"There's still time to change your mind," I suggested.

"What makes you say that?"

"I feel that you are afraid of letting me know. You are so upset."

"I am upset for a very different reason."

"Why?"

"Because I too am going to see."

"But you have done so already."

"One always sees new things, Victorien; that's the terrifying part of it."

I took hold of the curtain.

"Don't touch it, don't touch it!" he cried. "No one has the right, except myself. Who knows what would happen if any one except me were to open the closed door! Stand back, Victorien. Take up your position at two paces from the wall, a little to one side.... And now look!"

His voice was vibrant with energy and implacable determination. His expression was that of a man facing death; and, suddenly, with a single movement, he drew the black-serge curtain.

My emotion, I am certain, was just as great as Noël Dorgeroux's and my heart beat no less violently. My curiosity had reached its utmost bounds; moreover, I had a formidable intuition that I was about to enter into a region of mystery of which nothing, not even my uncle's disconcerting words, was able to give me the remotest idea. I was experiencing the contagion of what seemed to me in him to be a diseased condition; and I vainly strove to subject it in myself to the control of my reason. I was taking the impossible and the incredible for granted beforehand.

And yet I saw nothing at first; and there was, in fact, nothing. This part of the wall was bare. The only detail worthy of remark was that it was not vertical and that the whole base of the wall had been thickened so as to form a slightly inclined plane which sloped upwards to a height of nine feet. What was the reason for this work, when the wall did not need strengthening?

A coating of dark grey plaster, about half an inch thick, covered the whole panel. When closely examined, however, it was not painted over, but was rather a layer of some substance uniformly spread and showing no trace of a brush. Certain gleams proved that this layer was quite recent, like a varnish newly applied. I observed nothing else; and Heaven knows that I did my utmost to discover any peculiarity!

"Well, uncle?" I asked.

"Wait," he said, in an agonized voice, "wait! ... The first indication is beginning."

"What indication?"

"In the middle ... like a diffused light. Do you see it?"

"Yes, yes, I think I do."

It was as when a little daylight is striving to mingle with the waning darkness. A lighter disk became marked in the middle of the panel; and this lighter shade spread towards the edges, while remaining more intense at its centre. So far there was no very decided manifestation of anything out of the way; the chemical reaction of a substance lately hidden by the curtain and now exposed to the daylight and the sun was quite enough to explain this sort of inner illumination. Yet something gave one the haunting though perhaps unreasonable impression that an extraordinary phenomenon was about to take place. For that was what I expected, as did my uncle Dorgeroux.

And all at once he, who knew the premonitory symptoms and the course of the phenomenon, started, as though he had received a shock.

At the same moment, the thing happened.

It was sudden, instantaneous. It leapt in a flash from the depths

13

of the wall. Yes, I know, a spectacle cannot flash out of a wall, any more than it can out of a layer of dark-grey substance only half an inch thick. But I am setting down the sensation which I experienced, which is the same that hundreds and hundreds of people experienced afterwards, with a like clearness and a like certainty. It is no use carping at the undeniable fact: the thing shot out of the depths of the ocean of matter and it appeared violently, like the rays of a lighthouse flashing from the very womb of the darkness. After all, when we step towards a mirror, does our image not appear to us from the depth of that horizon suddenly unveiled?

Only, you see, it was not our image, my uncle Dorgeroux's or mine. Nothing was reflected, because there was nothing to reflect and no reflecting screen. What I saw was . . .

On the panel were "three geometrical figures which might equally well have been badly described circles or triangles composed of curved circles. In the centre of these figures was drawn a regular circle, marked in the middle with a blacker point, as the iris is marked by the pupil."

I am deliberately using the terminology which I employed to describe the images which my uncle had drawn in red chalk on the plaster of my room, for I had no doubt that he was then trying to reproduce those same figures, the appearance of which had already upset him.

"That's what you saw, isn't it, uncle?" I asked.

"Oh," he replied, in a low voice, "I saw much more than that, very much more! ... Wait and look right into them."

I stared wildly at the three "triangular circles," as I have called them. One of them was set above the two others; and these two, which were smaller and less regular but exactly alike, seemed, instead of looking straight before them, to turn a little to the right and to the left. Where did they come from? And what did they mean?

"Look," repeated my uncle. "Do you see?"

"Yes, yes," I replied, with a shudder. "The thing's moving."

It was in fact moving. Or rather, no, it was not: the outlines of the geometrical figures remained stationary; and not a line shifted its place within. And yet from all this immobility something emerged which was nothing else than motion.

I now remembered my uncle's words:

"They're alive, aren't they? You can see them opening and showing alarm! They're alive!"

They were alive! The three triangles were alive! And, as soon as I experienced this precise and undeniable feeling that they were alive, I ceased to regard them as an assemblage of lifeless lines and

14

began to see in them things which were like a sort of eyes, misshapen eyes, eyes different from ours, but eyes furnished with irises and pupils and throbbing in an abysmal darkness.

"They are looking at us!" I cried, quite beside myself and as feverish and unnerved as my uncle.

He nodded his head and whispered:

"Yes, that's what they're doing."

The three eyes were looking at us. We were conscious of the scrutiny of those three eyes, without lids or lashes, but full of an intense life which was due to the expression that animated them, a changing expression, by turns serious, proud, noble, enthusiastic and, above all, sad, grievously sad.

I feel how improbable these observations must appear. Nevertheless they correspond most strictly with the reality as it was beheld at a later date by the crowds that thronged to Haut-Meudon Lodge. Like my uncle, like myself, those crowds shuddered before three combinations of motionless lines which had the most heart-rending expression, just as at other moments they laughed at the comical or gayer expression which they were compelled to read into those same lines.

And on each occasion the spectacle which I am now describing was repeated in exactly the same order. A brief pause, followed by a series of vibrations. Then, suddenly, three eclipses, after which the combination of three triangles began to turn upon itself, as a whole, slowly at first and then with increasing rapidity, which gradually became transformed into so swift a rotation that one distinguished nothing but a motionless rose-pattern.

After that, nothing. The panel was empty.

CHAPTER III

AN EXECUTION

It must be understood that, notwithstanding the explanations which I must needs offer, the development of all these events took but very little time: exactly eighteen seconds, as I had the opportunity of calculating afterwards. But, during these eighteen seconds—and this again I observed on many an occasion—the spectator received the illusion of watching a complete drama, with its preliminary expositions, its plot and its culmination. And when this obscure, illogical drama was over, you questioned what you had seen, just as you question the nightmare which wakes you from your sleep.

Nevertheless it must be said that none of all this partook in any way of those absurd optical illusions which are so easily contrived or of those arbitrary ideas on which a whole pseudo-scientific novel is sometimes built up. There is no question of a novel, but of a physical phenomenon, an absolutely natural phenomenon, the explanation of which, when it comes to be known, is also absolutely natural.

And I beg those who are not acquainted with this explanation not to try to guess it. Let them not worry themselves with suppositions and interpretations. Let them forget, one by one, the theories over which I myself am lingering: all that has to do with B-rays, materializations, or the effect of solar heat. These are so many roads that lead nowhere. The best plan is to be guided by events, to have faith and to wait.

"It's finished, uncle, isn't it?" I asked.

"It's the beginning," he replied.

"How do you mean? The beginning of what? What's going to happen?"

"I don't know."

I was astounded:

"You don't know? But you knew just now, about this, about those strange eyes! ..."

"It all starts with that. But other things come afterwards, things which vary and which I know nothing about!"

"But how can that be possible?" I asked. "Do you mean to say that you don't know anything about them, you who prepared everything for them?"

"I prepared them, but I do not control them. As I told you, I

16

have opened a door which leads into the darkness; and from that darkness unforeseen images emerge."

"But is the thing that's coming of the same nature as those eyes?"

"No."

"Then what is it, uncle?"

"The thing that's coming will be a representation of images in conformity with what we are accustomed to see."

"Things which we shall understand, therefore?"

"Yes, we shall understand them; and yet they will be all the more incomprehensible."

I often wondered, during the weeks that followed, if my uncle's words were to be fully relied upon and if he had not uttered them in order to mislead me as to the origin and meaning of his discoveries. How indeed was it possible to think that the key to the riddle remained unknown to him? But at that moment I was wholly under his influence, steeped in the great mystery that surrounded us; and, with a constricted feeling at my heart, with all my overstimulated senses, I thought of nothing but gazing into the miraculous panel.

A movement on my uncle's part warned me. I gave a start. The dawn was rising over the grey surface.

I saw, first of all, a cloudy radiance whirling around a central point, towards which all the luminous spirals rushed and in which they were swallowed up while whirling upon themselves. Next, this point expanded into an ever wider circle, covered with a light, hazy veil which gradually dispersed, revealing a vague, floating image, like the apparitions raised by spiritualists and mediums at their sittings.

Then followed as it were a certain hesitation. The phantom image was striving with the diffuse shadow and seeking to attain life and light. Certain features became more pronounced. Outlines and separate planes took shape; and at last a flood of light issued from the phantom image and turned it into a dazzling picture, which seemed to be bathed in sunlight.

It was a woman's face.

I remember that at that moment my mental confusion was such that I felt like darting forward to feel the marvellous wall and lay my hands upon the living material in which the incredible phenomenon was vibrating. But my uncle dug his fingers into my arm:

"I won't have you move!" he growled. "If you budge an inch, the whole thing will fade away. Look!"

I did not move; indeed, I doubt whether I could have done so. My legs were giving way beneath me. Both of us, my uncle and I, dropped into a sitting posture on the fallen trunk of a tree.

17

"Look, look!" he commanded.

The woman's face had approached in our direction until it was twice the size of life. The first thing that struck us was the cap, which was that of a nurse, with the head-band tightly drawn over the forehead and the veil around the head. The features, handsome and regular and still young, wore that look of almost divine dignity which the primitive painters used to give to the saints who are suffering or about to suffer martyrdom, a nobility compounded of pain and ecstasy, of resignation and hope, of smiles and tears. Bathed in that light which really seemed to be an inward flame, the woman opened, upon a scene invisible to us, a pair of large dark eyes which, though filled with nameless terror, nevertheless were not afraid. The contrast was remarkable: her resignation was defiant; her fear was full of pride.

"Oh," stammered my uncle, "I seem to observe the same expression as in the Three Eyes which were there just now. Do you see: the same dignity, the same gentleness ... and also the same dread?"

"Yes," I replied, "it's the same expression, the same sequence of expressions."

And, while I spoke and while the woman still remained in the foreground, outside the frame of the picture, I felt certain recollections arise within me, as at the sight of the portrait of a person whose features are not entirely unfamiliar. My uncle received the same impression, for he said:

"I seem to remember ..."

But at that moment the strange face withdrew to the plane which it occupied at first. The mists that created a halo round it, drifted away. The shoulders came into view, followed by the whole body. We now saw a woman standing, fastened by bonds that gripped her bust and waist to a post the upper end of which rose a trifle above her head.

Then all this, which hitherto had given the impression of fixed outlines, like the outlines of a photograph, for instance, suddenly became alive, like a picture developing into a reality, a statue stepping straight into life. The bust moved. The arms, tied behind, and the imprisoned shoulders were struggling against the cords that were hurting them. The head turned slightly. The lips spoke. It was no longer an image presented for us to gaze at: it was life, moving and living life. It was a scene taking place in space and time. A whole background came into being, filled with people moving to and fro. Other figures were writhing, bound to posts. I counted eight of them. A squad of soldiers marched up, with shouldered rifles. They wore spiked helmets.

My uncle observed:

"Edith Cavell."

"Yes," I said, with a start, "I recognize her: Edith Cavell; the execution of Edith Cavell."

Once more and not for the last time, in setting down such phrases as these, I realize how ridiculous they must sound to any one who does not know to begin with what they signify and what is the exact truth that lies hidden in them. Nevertheless, I declare that this idea of something absurd and impossible did not occur to the mind when it was confronted with the phenomenon. Even when no theory had as yet suggested the smallest element of a logical explanation, people accepted as irrefutable the evidence of their own eyes. All those who saw the thing and whom I questioned gave me the same answer. Afterwards, they would correct themselves and protest. Afterwards, they would plead the excuse of hallucinations or visions received by suggestion. But, at the time, even though their reason was up in arms and though they, so to speak, "kicked" against facts which had no visible cause, they were compelled to bow before them and to follow their development as they would the representation of a succession of real events.

A theatrical representation, if you like, or rather a cinematographic representation, for, on the whole, this was the impression that emerged most clearly from all the impressions received. The moment Miss Cavell's image had assumed the animation of life, I turned round to look for the apparatus, standing in some corner of the Yard, which was projecting that animated picture; and, though I saw nothing, though I at once understood that in any case no projection could be effected in broad daylight and without omitting shafts of light, yet I received and retained that justifiable impression. There was no projector, no, but there was a screen: an astonishing screen which received nothing from without, since nothing was transmitted, but which received everything from within. And that was really the sensation experienced. The images did not come from the outside. They sprang to the surface from within. The horizon opened out on the farther side of a solid material. The darkness gave forth light.

Words, words, I know! Words which I heap upon words before I venture to write those which express what I saw issuing from the abyss in which Miss Cavell was about to undergo the death-penalty. The execution of Miss Cavell! Of course I said to myself, if it was a cinematographic representation, if it was a film—and how could one doubt it?—at any rate it was a film like ever so many others, faked, fictitious, based upon tradition, in a conventional setting, with paid performers and a heroine who had thoroughly studied the part. I

19

knew that. But, all the same, I watched as though I did not know it. The miracle of the spectacle was so great that one was constrained to believe in the whole miracle, that is to say, in the reality of the representation. No fake was here. No make-believe. No part learned by heart. No performers and no setting. It was the actual scene. The actual victims. The horror which thrilled me during those few minutes was that which I should have felt had I beheld the murderous dawn of the 8th of October, 1915, rise across the thrice-accursed drill-ground.

It was soon over. The firing-platoon was drawn up in double file, on the right and a little aslant, so that we saw the men's faces between the rifle-barrels. There were a good many of them: thirty, forty perhaps, forty butchers, booted, belted, helmeted, with their straps under their chins. Above them hung a pale sky, streaked with thin red clouds. Opposite them ... opposite them were the eight doomed victims.

There were six men and two women, all belonging to the people or the lower middle-class. They were now standing erect, throwing forward their chests as they tugged at their bonds.

An officer advanced, followed by four Feldwebel carrying unfurled handkerchiefs. Not any of the people condemned to death consented to have their eyes bandaged. Nevertheless, their faces were wrung with anguish; and all, with an impulse of their whole being, seemed to rush forward to their doom.

The officer raised his sword. The soldiers took aim.

A supreme effort of emotion seemed to add to the stature of the victims: and a cry issued from their lips. Oh, I saw and heard that cry, a fanatical and desperate cry in which the martyrs shouted forth their triumphant faith.

The officer's arm fell smartly. The intervening space appeared to tremble as with the rumbling of thunder. I had not the courage to look; and my eyes fixed themselves on the distracted countenance of Edith Cavell.

She also was not looking. Her eyelids were closed. But how she was listening! How her features contracted under the clash of the atrocious sounds, words of command, detonations, cries of the victims, death-rattles, moans of agony. By what refinement of cruelty had her own end been delayed? Why was she condemned to that double torture of seeing others die before dying herself?

Still, everything must be over yonder. One party of the butchers attended to the corpses, while the others formed into line and, pivoting upon the officer, marched towards Miss Cavell. They thus stepped out of the frame within which we were able to follow their movements; but I was able to perceive, by the gestures of the officer, that they were forming up opposite Nurse Cavell, between her and us.

The officer stepped towards her, accompanied by a military chaplain, who placed a crucifix to her lips. She kissed it fervently and tenderly. The chaplain then gave her his blessing; and she was left alone. A mist once more shrouded the scene, leaving her whole figure full in the light. Her eyelids were still closed, her head erect and her body rigid.

She was at that moment wearing a very sweet and very tranquil expression. Not a trace of fear distorted her noble countenance. She stood awaiting death with saintly serenity.

And this death, as it was revealed to us, was neither very cruel nor very odious. The upper part of the body fell forward. The head drooped a little to one side. But the shame of it lay in what followed. The officer stood close to the victim, revolver in hand. And he was pressing the barrel to his victim's temple, when, suddenly, the mist broke into dense waves and the whole picture disappeared. . . .

CHAPTER IV

NOËL DORGEROUX'S SON

The spectator who has just been watching the most tragic of films finds it easy to escape from the sort of dark prison-house in which he was suffocating and, with the return of the light, recovers his equilibrium and his self-possession. I, on the other hand, remained for a long time numb and speechless, with my eyes riveted to the empty panel, as though I expected something else to emerge from it. Even when it was over, the tragedy terrified me, like a nightmare prolonged after waking, and, even more than the tragedy, the absolutely extraordinary manner in which it had been unfolded before my eyes. I did not understand. My disordered brain vouchsafed me none but the most grotesque and incoherent ideas.

A movement on the part of Noël Dorgeroux drew me from my stupor: he had drawn the curtain across the screen.

At this I vehemently seized my uncle by his two hands and cried:

"What does all this mean? It's maddening! What explanation are you able to give?"

"None," he said, simply.

"But still ... you brought me here."

"Yes, that you might also see and to make sure that my eyes had not deceived me."

"Therefore you have already witnessed other scenes in that same setting?"

"Yes, other sights ... three times before."

"What, uncle? Can you specify them?"

"Certainly: what I saw yesterday, for instance."

"What was that, uncle?"

He pushed me a little and gazed at me, at first without replying. Then, speaking in a very low tone, with deliberate conviction, he said:

"The battle of Trafalgar."

I wondered if he was making fun of me. But Noël Dorgeroux was little addicted to banter at any time; and he would not have selected such a moment as this to depart from his customary gravity. No, he was speaking seriously; and what he said suddenly struck me as so humorous that I burst out laughing:

"Trafalgar! Don't be offended, uncle; but it's really too quaint! The battle of Trafalgar, which was fought in 1805?"

22

He once more looked at me attentively:

"Why do you laugh?" he asked.

"Good heavens, I laugh, I laugh ... because ... well, confess ..."

He interrupted me:

"You're laughing for very simple reasons, Victorien, which I will explain to you in a few words. To begin with, you are nervous and ill at ease; and your merriment is first and foremost a reaction. But, in addition, the spectacle of that horrible scene was so—what shall I say?—so convincing that you looked upon it, in spite of yourself, not as a reconstruction of the murder, but as the actual murder of Miss Cavell. Is that true?"

"Perhaps it is, uncle."

"In other words, the murder and all the infamous details which accompanied it must have been—don't let us hesitate to use the word—must have been cinematographed by some unseen witness from whom I obtained that precious film: and my invention consists solely in reproducing the film in the thickness of a gelatinous layer of some kind or other. A wonderful, but a credible discovery. Are we still agreed?"

"Yes, uncle, quite."

"Very well. But now I am claiming something very different. I am claiming to have witnessed an evocation of the battle of Trafalgar! If so, the French and English frigates must have foundered before my eyes! I must have seen Nelson die, struck down at the foot of his mainmast! That's quite another matter, is it not? In 1805 there were no cinematographic films. Therefore this can be only an absurd parody. Thereupon all your emotion vanishes. My reputation fades into thin air. And you laugh! I am to you nothing more than an old impostor, who, instead of humbly showing you his curious discovery, tries in addition to persuade you that the moon is made of green cheese! A humbug, what?"

We had left the wall and were walking towards the door of the garden. The sun was setting behind the distant hills. I stopped and said to Noël Dorgeroux:

"Forgive me, uncle, and please don't think that I am over lacking in the respect I owe you. There is nothing in my amusement that need annoy you, nothing to make you suppose that I suspect your absolute sincerity."

"Then what do you think? What is your conclusion?"

"I don't think anything, uncle. I have arrived at no conclusion and I am not even trying to do so, at present. I am out of my depth, perplexed, at the same time dazed and dissatisfied, as though I felt that the riddle was even more wonderful than it is and that it would always remain insoluble."

We were entering the garden. It was his turn to stop me:

"Insoluble! That is really your opinion?"

"Yes, for the moment."

"You can't imagine any theory?"

"No."

"Still, you saw? You have no doubts?"

"I certainly saw. I saw first three strange eyes that looked at us; then I witnessed a scene which was the murder of Miss Cavell. That is what I saw, just as you did, uncle; and I do not for a moment doubt the undeniable evidence of my own eyes."

He held out his hand to me:

"That's what I wanted to know, my boy. And thank you."

I have given a faithful account of what happened that afternoon. In the evening we dined together by ourselves, Bérangère having sent word to say that she was indisposed and would not leave her room. My uncle was deeply absorbed in thought and did not say a word on what had happened in the Yard.

I slept hardly at all, haunted by the recollection of what I had seen and tormented by a score of theories, which I need not mention here, for not one of them was of the slightest value.

Next day, Bérangère did not come downstairs. At luncheon, my uncle preserved the same silence. I tried many times to make him talk, but received no reply.

My curiosity was too intense to allow my uncle to get rid of me in this way. I took up my position in the garden before he left the house. Not until five o'clock did he go up to the Yard.

"Shall I come with you, uncle?" I suggested, boldly.

He grunted, neither granting my request nor refusing it. I followed him. He walked across the Yard, locked himself into his principal workshop and did not leave it until an hour later:

"Ah, there you are!" he said, as though he had been unaware of any presence.

He went to the wall and briskly drew the curtain. Just then he asked me to go back to the workshop and to fetch something or other which he had forgotten. When I returned, he said, excitedly:

"It's finished, it's finished!"

"What is, uncle?"

"The Eyes, the Three Eyes."

"Oh, have you seen them?"

"Yes; and I refuse to believe ... no, of course, it's an illusion on my part.... How could it be possible, when you come to think of it? Imagine, the eyes wore the expression of my dead son's eyes, yes, the very expression of my poor Dominique. It's madness, isn't it? And yet I declare, yes, I declare that Dominique was gazing at me ...

at first with a sad and sorrowful gaze, which suddenly became the terrified gaze of a man who is staring death in the face. And then the Three Eyes began to revolve upon themselves. That was the end."

I made Noël Dorgeroux sit down:

"It's as you suppose, uncle, an illusion, an hallucination. Just think, Dominique has been dead so many years! It is therefore incredible ..."

"Everything is incredible and nothing is," he said. "There is no room for human logic in front of that wall."

I tried to reason with him, though my mind was becoming as bewildered as his own. But he silenced me:

"That'll do," he said. "Here's the other thing beginning."

He pointed to the screen, which was showing signs of life and preparing to reveal a new picture.

"But, uncle," I said, already overcome by excitement, "where does that come from?"

"Don't speak," said Noël Dorgeroux. "Not a word."

I at once observed that this other thing bore no relation to what I had witnessed the day before; and I concluded that the scenes presented must occur without any prearranged order, without any chronological or serial connection, in short, like the different films displayed in the course of a performance.

It was the picture of a small town as seen from a neighbouring height. A castle and a church-steeple stood out above it. The town was built on the slope of several hills and at the intersection of the valleys, which met among clumps of tall, leafy trees.

Suddenly, it came nearer and was seen on a larger scale. The hills surrounding the town disappeared; and the whole screen was filled with a crowd swarming with lively gestures around an open space above which hung a balloon, held captive by ropes. Suspended from the balloon was a receptacle serving probably for the production of hot air. Men were issuing from the crowd on every hand. Two of them climbed a ladder the top of which was leaning against the side of a car. And all this, the appearance of the balloon, the shape of the appliances employed, the use of hot air instead of gas, the dress of the people; all this struck me as possessing an old-world aspect.

"The brothers Montgolfier," whispered my uncle.

These few words enlightened me. I remembered those old prints recording man's first ascent towards the sky, which was accomplished in June, 1783. It was this wonderful event which we were witnessing, or, at least, I should say, a reconstruction of the event, a reconstruction accurately based upon those old prints, with a balloon copied from the original, with costumes of the period and no doubt, in addition, the actual setting of the little town of Annonay.

But then how was it that there was so great a multitude of townsfolk and peasants? There was no comparison possible between the usual number of actors in a cinema scene and the incredibly tight-packed crowd which I saw moving before my eyes. A crowd like that is found only in pictures which the camera has secured direct, on a public holiday, at a march-past of troops or a royal procession.

However, the wavelike eddying of the crowd suddenly subsided. I received the impression of a great silence and an anxious period of waiting. Some men quickly severed the ropes with hatchets. Etienne and Joseph Montgolfier lifted their hats.

And the balloon rose in space. The people in the crowd raised their arms and filled the air with an immense clamour.

For a moment, the screen showed us the two brothers, by themselves and enlarged. With the upper part of their bodies leaning from the car, each with one arm round the other's waist and one hand clasping the other's, they seemed to be praying with an air of unspeakable ecstasy and solemn joy.

Slowly the ascent continued. And it was then that something utterly inexplicable occurred: the balloon, as it rose above the little town and the surrounding hills, did not appear to my uncle and me as an object which we were watching from an increasing depth below. No, it was the little town and the hills which were sinking and which, by sinking, proved to us that the balloon was ascending. But there was also this absolutely illogical phenomenon, that we remained on the same level as the balloon, that it retained the same dimensions and that the two brothers stood facing us, exactly as though the photograph had been taken from the car of a second balloon, rising at the same time as the first with an exactly and mathematically identical movement!

The scene was not completed. Or rather it was transformed in accordance with the method of the cinematograph, which substitutes one picture for another by first blending them together. Imperceptibly, when it was perhaps some fifteen hundred feet from the ground, the Montgolfier balloon became less distinct and its vague and softened outlines gradually mingled with the more and more powerful outlines of another shape which soon occupied the whole space and which proved to be that of a military aeroplane.

Several times since then the mysterious screen has shown me two successive scenes of which the second completed the first, thus forming a diptych which displayed the evident wish to convey a lesson by connecting, across space and time, two events which in this way acquired their full significance. This time the moral was clear: the peaceable balloon had culminated in the murderous aeroplane. First the ascent at Annonay. Then a fight in mid-air, a fight between the monoplane which I had seen develop from the old-fashioned balloon and the biplane upon which I beheld it swooping like a bird of prey.

Was it an illusion or a "faked representation?" For here again we saw the two aeroplanes not in the normal fashion, from below, but as if we were at the same height and moving at the same rate of speed. In that case, were we to admit that an operator, perched on a third machine, was calmly engaged in "filming" the shifting fortunes of the terrible battle? That was impossible, surely!

But there was no good purpose to be served by renewing these perpetual suppositions over and over again. Why should I doubt the unimpeachable evidence of my eyes and deny the undeniable? Real aeroplanes were manoeuvring before my eyes. A real fight was taking place in the thickness of that old wall.

It did not last long. The man who was alone was attacking boldly. Time after time his machine-gun flashed forth flames. Then, to avoid the enemy's bullets, he looped the loop twice, each time throwing his aeroplane in such a position that I was able to distinguish on the canvas the three concentric circles that denote the Allied machines. Then, coming nearer and attacking his adversaries from behind, he returned to his gun.

The Hun biplane—I observed the iron cross—dived straight for the ground and recovered itself. The two men seemed to be sitting tight under their furs and masks. There was a third machine-gun attack. The pilot threw up his hands. The biplane capsized and fell.

I saw this fall in the most inexplicable fashion. At first, of course, it seemed swift as lightning. And then it became infinitely slow and even ceased, with the machine overturned and the two bodies motionless, head downwards and arms outstretched.

Then the ground shot up with a dizzy speed, devastated, shell-holed fields, swarming with thousands of French poilus.

The biplane came down beside a river. From the shapeless fuselage and the shattered wings two legs appeared.

And the French plane landed almost immediately, a short way off. The victor stepped out, pushed back the soldiers who had run up from every side and, moving a few yards towards his motionless prey, took off his mask and made the sign of the cross.

"Oh," I whispered, "this is dreadful! And how mysterious! ..."

Then I saw that Noël Dorgeroux was on his knees, his face distorted with emotion:

"What is it, uncle?" I asked.

27

Stretching towards the wall his trembling hands, which were clasped together, he stammered:

"Dominique! I recognize my son! It's he! Oh, I'm terrified!"

I also, as I gazed at the victor, recovered in my memory the time-effaced image of my poor cousin.

"It's he!" continued my uncle. "I was right ... the expression of the Three Eyes.... Oh! I can't look! ... I'm afraid!"

"Afraid of what, uncle?"

"They are going to kill him ... to kill him before my eyes ... to kill him as they actually did kill him ... Dominique! Dominique! Take care!" he shouted.

I did not shout: what warning cry could reach the man about to die? But the same terror brought me to my knees and made me wring my hands. In front of us, from underneath the shapeless mass, among the heaped-up wreckage, something rose up, the swaying body of one of the victims. An arm was extended, aiming a revolver. The victor sprang to one side. It was too late. Shot through the head, he spun round upon his heels and fell beside the dead body of his murderer.

The tragedy was over.

My uncle, bent double, was sobbing pitifully a few paces from my side. He had witnessed the actual death of his son, foully murdered in the great war by a German airman!

CHAPTER V

THE KISS

Bérangère next day resumed her place at meals, looking a little pale and wearing a more serious face than usual. My uncle, who had not troubled about her during the last two days, kissed her absent-mindedly. We lunched without a word. Not until we had nearly ended did Noël Dorgeroux speak to his god-child:

"Well, dear, are you none the worse for your fall?"

"Not a bit, god-father; and I'm only sorry that I didn't see ... what you saw up there, yesterday and the day before. Are you going there presently, god-father?"

"Yes, but I'm going alone."

This was said in a peremptory tone which allowed of no reply. My uncle was looking at me. I did not stir a muscle.

Lunch finished in an awkward silence. As he was about to leave the room, Noël Dorgeroux turned back to me and asked:

"Do you happen to have lost anything in the Yard?"

"No, uncle. Why do you ask?"

"Because," he answered, with a slight hesitation, "because I found this on the ground, just in front of the wall."

He showed me a lens from an eye-glass.

"But you know, uncle," I said, laughing, "that I don't wear spectacles or glasses of any kind."

"No more do I!" Bérangère declared.

"That's so, that's so," Noël Dorgeroux replied, in a thoughtful tone. "But, still, somebody has been there. And you can understand my uneasiness."

In the hope of making him speak, I pursued the subject:

"What are you uneasy about, uncle? At the worst, some one may have seen the pictures produced on the screen, which would not be enough, so it seems to me, to enable the secret of your discovery to be stolen. Remember that I myself, who was with you, am hardly any wiser than I was before."

I felt that he did not intend to answer and that he resented my insistence. This irritated me.

"Listen, uncle," I said. "Whatever the reasons for your conduct may be, you have no right to suspect me; and I ask and entreat you to give me an explanation. Yes, I entreat you, for I cannot remain in this uncertainty. Tell me, uncle, was it really your son whom you saw die, or were we shown a fabricated picture of his death? Then

29

again, what is the unseen and omnipotent entity which causes these phantoms to follow one another in that incredible magic lantern? Never was there such a problem, never so many irreconcilable questions. Look here, last night, while I was trying for hours to get to sleep, I imagined—it's an absurd theory, I know, but, all the same, one has to cast about—well, I remembered that you had spoken to Bérangère of a certain inner force which radiated from us and emitted what you have named the B-rays, after your god-daughter. If so, might one not suppose that, in the circumstances, this force, emanating, uncle, from your own brain, which was haunted by a vague resemblance between the expression of the Three Eyes and the expression of your own, might we not suppose that this force projected on the receptive material of the wall the scene which was conjured up in your mind? Don't you think that the screen which you have covered with a special substance registered your thoughts just as a sensitive plate, acted upon by the sunlight, registers forms and outlines? In that case ..."

I broke off. As I spoke, the words which I was using seemed to me devoid of meaning. My uncle, however, appeared to be listening to them with a certain willingness and even to be waiting for what I would say next. But I did not know what to say. I had suddenly come to the end of my tether; and, though I made every effort to detain Noël Dorgeroux by fresh arguments, I felt that there was not a word more to be said between us on that subject.

Indeed, my uncle went away without answering one of my questions. I saw him, through the window, crossing the garden.

I gave way to a movement of anger and exclaimed to Bérangère:

"I've had enough of this! After all, why should I worry myself to death trying to understand a discovery which, when you think of it, is not a discovery at all? For what does it consist of? No one can respect Noël Dorgeroux more than I do; but there's no doubt that this, instead of a real discovery, is rather a stupefying way of deluding one's self, of mixing up things that exist with things that do not exist and of giving an appearance of reality to what has none. Unless ... But who knows anything about it? It is not even possible to express an opinion. The whole thing is an ocean of mystery, overhung by mountainous clouds which descend upon one and stifle one!"

My ill-humour suddenly turned against Bérangère. She had listened to me with a look of disapproval, feeling angry perhaps at my blaming her god-father; and she was now slipping towards the door. I stopped her as she was passing; and, in a fit of rancour which was foreign to my nature, I let fly:

"Why are you leaving the room? Why do you always avoid me

30

as you do? Speak, can't you? What have you against me? Yes, I know, my thoughtless conduct, the other day. But do you think I would have acted like that if you weren't always keeping up that sulky reserve with me? Hang it all, I've known you as quite a little girl! I've held your skipping-rope for you when you were just a slip of a child! Then why should I now be made to look on you as a woman and to feel that you are indeed a woman ... a woman who stirs me to the very depths of my heart?"

She was standing against the door and gazing at me with an undefinable smile, which contained a gleam of mockery, but nothing provocative and not a shade of coquetry. I noticed for the first time that her eyes, which I thought to be grey, were streaked with green and, as it were, flecked with specks of gold. And, at the same time, the expression of those great eyes, bright and limpid though they were, struck me as the most unfathomable thing in the world. What was passing in those limpid depths? And why did my mind connect the riddle of those eyes with the terrible riddle which the three geometrical eyes had set me?

However, the recollection of the stolen kiss diverted my glance to her red lips. Her face turned crimson. This was a last, exasperating insult.

"Let me be! Go away!" she commanded, quivering with anger and shame.

Helpless and a prisoner, she lowered her head and bit her lips to prevent my seeing them. Then, when I tried to take her hands, she thrust her outstretched arms against my chest, pushed me back with all her might and cried:

"You're a mean coward! Go away! I loathe and hate you!"

Her outburst restored my composure. I was ashamed of what I had done and, making way for her to pass, I opened the door for her and said:

"I beg your pardon, Bérangère. Don't be angrier with me than you can help. I promise you it shan't occur again."

Once more, the story of the Three Eyes is closely bound up with all the details of my love, not only in my recollection of it, but also in actual fact. While the riddle itself is alien to it and may be regarded solely in its aspect of a scientific phenomenon, it is impossible to describe how humanity came to know of it and was brought into immediate contact with it, without at the same time revealing all the vicissitudes of my sentimental adventure. The riddle and this adventure, from the point of view with which we are concerned, are integral parts of the same whole. The two must be described simultaneously.

At the moment, being somewhat disillusionized in both

respects, I decided to tear myself away from this twofold preoccupation and to leave my uncle to his inventions and Bérangère to her sullen mood.

I had not much difficulty in carrying out my resolve in so far as Noël Dorgeroux was concerned. We had a long succession of wet days. The rain kept him to his room or his laboratories; and the pictures on the screen faded from my mind like diabolical visions which the brain refuses to accept. I did not wish to think of them; and I thought of them hardly at all.

But Bérangère's charm pervaded me, notwithstanding the good faith in which I waged this daily battle. Unaccustomed to the snares of love, I fell an easy prey, incapable of defence. Bérangère's voice, her laugh, her silence, her day-dreams, her way of holding herself, the fragrance of her personality, the colour of her hair served me as so many excuses for exaltation, rejoicing, suffering or despair. Through the breach now opened in my professorial soul, which hitherto had known few joys save those of study, came surging all the feelings that make up the delights and also the pangs of love, all the emotions of longing, hatred, fondness, fear, hope ... and jealousy.

It was one bright and peaceful morning, as I was strolling in the Meudon woods, that I caught sight of Bérangère in the company of a man. They were standing at a corner where two roads met and were talking with some vivacity. The man faced me. I saw a type of what would be described as a coxcomb, with regular features, a dark, fan-shaped beard and a broad smile which displayed his teeth. He wore a double eye-glass.

Bérangère heard the sound of my footsteps, as I approached, and turned round. Her attitude denoted hesitation and confusion. But she at once pointed down one of the two roads, as though giving a direction. The fellow raised his hat and walked away. Bérangère joined me and, without much restraint, explained:

"It was somebody asking his way."

"But you know him, Bérangère?" I objected.

"I never saw him before in my life," she declared.

"Oh, come, come! Why, from the manner you were speaking to him ... Look here, Bérangère, will you take your oath on it?"

She started:

"What do you mean? Why should I take an oath to you? I am not accountable to you for my actions."

"In that case, why did you tell me that he was enquiring his way of you? I asked you no question."

"I do as I please," she replied, curtly.

Nevertheless, when we reached the Lodge, she thought better of it and said:

"After all, if it gives you any pleasure, I can swear that I was seeing that gentleman for the first time and that I had never heard of him. I don't even know his name."

We parted.

"One word more," I said. "Did you notice that the man wore glasses?"

"So he did!" she said, with some surprise. "Well, what does that prove?"

"Remember, your uncle found a spectacle-lens in front of the wall in the Yard."

She stopped to think and then shrugged her shoulders:

"A mere coincidence! Why should you connect the two things?"

Bérangère was right and I did not insist. Nevertheless and though she had answered me in a tone of undeniable candour, the incident left me uneasy and suspicious. I would not admit that so animated a conversation could take place between her and a perfect stranger who was simply asking her the way. The man was well set-up and good-looking. I suffered tortures.

That evening Bérangère was silent. It struck me that she had been crying. My uncle, on the contrary, on returning from the Yard, was talkative and cheerful; and I more than once felt that he was on the point of telling me something. Had anything thrown fresh light on his invention?

Next day, he was just as lively:

"Life is very pleasant, at times," he said.

And he left us, rubbing his hands.

Bérangère spent all the early part of the afternoon on a bench in the garden, where I could see her from my room. She sat motionless and thoughtful.

At four o'clock, she came in, walked across the hall of the Lodge and went out by the front door.

I went out too, half a minute later.

The street which skirted the house turned and likewise skirted, on the left, the garden and the Yard, whereas on the right the property was bordered by a narrow lane which led to some fields and abandoned quarries. Bérangère often went this way; and I at once saw, by her slow gait, that her only intention was to stroll wherever her dreams might lead her.

She had not put on a hat. The sunlight gleamed in her hair. She picked the stones on which to place her feet, so as not to dirty her shoes with the mud in the road.

Against the stout plank fence which at this point replaced the wall enclosing the Yard stood an old street-lamp, now no longer used, which was fastened to the fence with iron clamps. Bérangère stopped here, all of a sudden, evidently in obedience to a thought which, I confess, had often occurred to myself and which I had had the courage to resist, perhaps because I had not perceived the means of putting it into execution.

Bérangère saw the means. It was only necessary to climb the fence by using the lamp, in order to make her way into the Yard without her uncle's knowledge and steal a glimpse of one of those sights which he guarded so jealously for himself.

She made up her mind without hesitation; and, when she was on the other side, I too had not the least hesitation in following her example. I was in that state of mind when one is not unduly troubled by idle scruples; and there was no more indelicacy in satisfying my legitimate curiosity than in spying upon Bérangère's actions. I therefore climbed over also.

My scruples returned when I found myself on the other side, face to face with Bérangère, who had experienced some difficulty in getting down. I said, a little sheepishly:

"This is not a very nice thing we're doing, Bérangère; and I presume you mean to give it up."

She began to laugh:

"You can give it up. I intend to go on. If god-father chooses to distrust us, it's his look-out."

I did not try to restrain her. She slipped softly between the nearest two sheds. I followed close upon her heels.

In this way we stole to the end of the open ground which occupied the middle of the Yard and we saw Noël Dorgeroux standing by the screen. He had not yet drawn the black-serge curtain.

"Look," Bérangère whispered, "over there: you see a stack of wood with a tarpaulin over it? We shall be all right behind that."

"But suppose my uncle looks round while we're crossing?"

"He won't."

She was the first to venture across; and I joined her without any mishap. We were not more than a dozen yards from the screen.

"My heart's beating so!" said Bérangère. "I've seen nothing, you know: only those—sort of eyes. And there's a lot more, isn't there?"

Our refuge consisted of two stacks of small short planks, with bags of sand between the stacks. We sat down here, in a position which brought us close together. Nevertheless Bérangère maintained the same distant attitude as before; and I now thought of nothing but what my uncle was doing.

He was holding his watch in his hand and consulting it at

intervals, as though waiting for a time which he had fixed beforehand. And that time arrived. The curtain grated on its metal rod. The screen was uncovered.

From where we sat we could see the bare surface as well as my uncle could, for the intervening space fell very far short of the length of an ordinary picture-palace. The first outlines to appear were therefore absolutely plain to us. They were the lines of the three geometrical figures which I knew so well: the same proportions, the same arrangement, the same impassiveness, followed by that same palpitation, coming entirely from within, which animated them and made them live.

"Yes, yes," whispered Bérangère, "my god-father said so one day: they are alive, the Three Eyes."

"They are alive," I declared, "and they gaze at you. Look at the two lower eyes by themselves; think of them as actual eyes; and you will see that they really have an expression. There, they're smiling now."

"You're right, they're smiling."

"And see what a soft and gentle look they have now ... a little serious also.... Oh, Bérangère, it's impossible!"

"What?"

"They have your expression, Bérangère, your expression."

"What nonsense! It's ridiculous!"

"The very expression of your eyes. You don't know it yourself. But I do. They have never looked at me like that; but, all the same, they are your eyes, it's their expression, their charm. I know, because these make me feel ... eh, as yours do, Bérangère!"

But the end was approaching. The three geometrical figures began to revolve upon themselves with the same dizzy motion which reduced them to a confused disk which soon vanished.

"They're your eyes, Bérangère," I stammered; "there's not a doubt about it; it was as though you were looking at me."

Yes, she had the same look; and I could not but remember then that Edith Cavell had also looked in that way at Noël Dorgeroux and me, through the three strange eyes, and that Noël Dorgeroux similarly had recognized the look in his son's eyes before his son himself appeared to him. That being so, was I to assume that each of the films—there is no other word for them—was preceded by the fabulous vision of three geometrical figures containing, captive and alive, the very expression in the eyes of one of the persons about to come to life upon the screen?

It was a lunatic assumption, as were all those which I was making! I blush to write it down. But, in that case, what were the

35

three geometrical figures? A cinema trade-mark? The trade-mark of the Three Eyes? What an absurdity! What madness! And yet . . .

"Oh," said Bérangère, making as if to rise, "I oughtn't to have come! It's suffocating me. Can you explain?"

"No, Bérangère, I can't. It's suffocating me too. Do you want to go?"

"No," she said, leaning forward. "No, I want to see."

And we saw. And, at the very moment when a muffled cry escaped our lips, we saw Noël Dorgeroux slowly making a great sign of the cross.

Opposite him, in the middle of the magic space on the wall, was he himself this time, standing not like a frail and shifting phantom, but like a human being full of movement and life. Yes, Noël Dorgeroux went to and fro before us and before himself, wearing his usual skull-cap, dressed in his long frock-coat. And the setting in which he moved was none other than the Yard, the Yard with its shed, its workshops, its disorder, its heaps of scrap-iron, its stacks of wood, its rows of barrels and its wall, with the rectangle of the serge curtain!

I at once noticed one detail: the serge curtain covered the magic space completely. It was therefore impossible to imagine that this scene, at any rate, had been recorded, absorbed by the screen, which, at that actual moment, must have drawn it from its own substance in order to present that sight to us! It was impossible, because Noël Dorgeroux had his back turned to the wall. It was impossible, because we saw the wall itself and the door of the garden, because the gate was open and because I, in my turn, entered the Yard.

"You! It's you!" gasped Bérangère.

"It's I on the day when your uncle told me to come here," I said, astounded, "the day when I first saw a vision on the screen."

At that moment, on the screen, Noël Dorgeroux beckoned to me from the door of his workshop. We went in together. The Yard remained empty; and then, after an eclipse which lasted only a second or two, the same scene reappeared, the little garden-door opened again and Bérangère, all smiles, put her head through. She seemed to be saying:

"Nobody here. They're in the office. Upon my word, I'll risk it!"

And she crept along the wall, towards the serge curtain.

All this happened quickly, without any of the vibration seen in the picture-theatres, and so clearly and plainly that I followed our two images not as the phases of an incident buried in the depths of time, but as the reflection in a mirror of a scene in which we were the immediate actors. To tell the truth, I was confused at seeing myself over there and feeling myself to be where I was. This doubling of my personality made my brain reel.

"Victorien," said Bérangère, in an almost inaudible voice, "you're going to come out of your uncle's workshop as you did the other day, aren't you?"

"Yes," I said, "the details of the other day are beginning all over again."

And they did. Here were my uncle and I coming out of the workshop. Here was Bérangère, surprised, running away and laughing. Here she was, climbing a plank lying across two barrels and dancing, ever so gracefully and lightly! And then, as before, she fell. I darted forward, picked her up, carried her and laid her on the bench. She put her arms round me; our faces almost touched. And, as before, gently at first and then roughly and violently, I kissed her on the lips. And, as on that occasion, she rose to her feet, while I crouched before her.

Oh, how well I remember it all! I remember and I still see myself. I see myself yonder, bending very low not daring to lift my head, and I see Bérangère, standing up, covered with shame, trembling with indignation.

Indignation? Did she really seem indignant? But then why did her dear face, the face on the screen, display such indulgence and gentleness? Why did she smile with that expression of unspeakable gladness? Yes, I swear it was gladness. Yonder, in the magic space where that exciting minute was being reenacted, there stood over me a happy creature who was gazing at me with joy and affection, who was gazing at me thus because she knew that I could not see her and because she could not know that one day I should see her.

"Bérangère! ... Bérangère! ..."

But suddenly, while the adorable vision yonder continued, my eyes were covered as with a veil. Bérangère had turned towards me and put her two hands over my eyes, whispering:

"Don't look. I won't have you look. Besides, it's not true. That woman's lying, it's not me at all.... No, no, I never looked at you like that."

Her voice grew fainter. Her hands dropped to her sides. And, with all the strength gone out of her, she let herself fall against my shoulder, gently and silently.

Ten minutes later, I went back alone. Bérangère had left me without a word, after her unexpected movement of surrender.

Next morning I received a telegram from the rector of the university, calling me to Grenoble. Bérangère did not appear as I was leaving. But, when my uncle brought me to the station, I saw her, not far from the Lodge, talking with that confounded coxcomb whom she pretended not to know.

CHAPTER VI

ANXIETIES

"You seem very happy, uncle!" said I to Noël Dorgeroux, who walked briskly on the way to the station, whistling one gay tune after another.

"Yes," he replied, "I am happy as a man is who has come to a decision."

"You've come to a decision, uncle?"

"And a very serious one at that. It has cost me a sleepless night; but it's worth it."

"May I ask ... ?"

"Certainly. In two words, it's this: I'm going to pull down the sheds in the Yard and build an amphitheatre there."

"What for?"

"To exploit the thing ... the thing you know of."

"How do you mean, to exploit it?"

"Why, it's a tremendously important discovery; and, if properly worked, it will give me the money which I have always been trying for, not for its own sake, but because of the resources which it will bring me, money with the aid of which I shall be able to continue my labours without being checked by secondary considerations. There are millions to be made, Victorien, millions! And what shall I not accomplish with millions! This brain of mine," he went on, tapping his forehead, "is simply crammed with ideas, with theories which need verifying. And it all takes money.... Money! Money! You know how little I care about money! But I want millions, if I am to carry through my work. And those millions I shall have!"

Mastering his enthusiasm, he took my arm and explained:

"First of all, the Yard cleared of its rubbish and levelled. After that, the amphitheatre, with five stages of benches facing the wall. For of course the wall remains: it is the essential point, the reason for the whole thing. But I shall heighten and widen it; and, when it is quite unobstructed, there will be a clear view of it from every seat. You follow me, don't you?"

"I follow you, uncle. But do you think people will come?"

"Will they come? What! You, who know, ask me that question! Why, they will pay gold for the worst seat, they'll give a king's ransom to get in! I'm so sure of it that I shall put all I have left, the last remnant of my savings, into the business. And within a year I shall have amassed incalculable wealth."

"The place is quite small, uncle, and you will have only a limited number of seats."

"A thousand, a thousand seats, comfortably! At two hundred francs a seat to begin with, at a thousand francs! ..."

"I say, uncle! Seats in the open air, exposed to the rain, to the cold, to all sorts of weather!"

"I've foreseen that objection. The Yard will be closed on rainy days. I want bright daylight, sunshine, the action of the light and other conditions besides, which will still further decrease the number of demonstrations. But that doesn't matter: each seat will cost two thousand francs, five thousand francs, if necessary! I tell you, there's no limit! No one will be content to die without having been to Noël Dorgeroux's Yard! Why, Victorien, you know it as well as I do! When all is said, the reality is more extraordinary than anything that you can imagine, even after what you have seen with your own eyes."

I could not help asking him:

"Then there are fresh manifestations?"

He replied by nodding his head:

"It's not so much that they're new," he said, "as that, above all, they have enabled me, with the factors which I already possess, to probe the truth to the bottom."

"Uncle! Uncle!" I cried. "You mean to say that you know the truth?"

"I know the whole truth, my boy," he declared. "I know how much is my work and how much has nothing to do with me. What was once darkness is now dazzling light."

And he added, in a very serious tone:

"It is beyond all imagination, my boy. It is beyond the most extravagant dreams; and yet it remains within the province of facts and certainties. Once humanity knows of it, the earth will pass through a thrill of religious awe; and the people who come here as pilgrims will fall upon their knees—as I did—fall upon their knees like children who pray and fold their hands and weep!"

His words, which were obviously exaggerated, seemed to come from an ill-balanced mind. Yet I felt the force of their exciting and feverish influence:

"Explain yourself, uncle, I beg you."

"Later on, my boy, when all the points have been cleared up."

"What are you afraid of?"

"Nothing from you."

"From whom then?"

"Nobody. But I have my misgivings ... quite wrongly, perhaps. Still, certain facts lead me to think that I am being spied upon and that some one is trying to discover my secret. It's just a few clues ... things that have been moved from their place ... and, above all, a vague intuition."

"This is all very indefinite, uncle."

"Very, I admit," he said, drawing himself up. "And so forgive me if my precautions are excessive ... and let's talk of something else: of yourself, Victorien, of your plans ..."

"I have no plans, uncle."

"Yes, you have. There's one at least that you're keeping from me."

"How so?"

He stopped in his walk and said:

"You're in love with Bérangère."

I did not think of protesting, knowing that Noël Dorgeroux had been in the Yard the day before, in front of the screen:

"I am, uncle, I'm in love with Bérangère, but she doesn't care for me."

"Yes, she does, Victorien."

I displayed some slight impatience:

"Uncle, I must ask you not to insist. Bérangère is a mere child; she does not know what she wants; she is incapable of any serious feeling; and I do not intend to think about her any more. On my part, it was just a fancy of which I shall soon be cured."

Noël Dorgeroux shrugged his shoulders:

"Lovers' quarrels! Now this is what I have to say to you, Victorien. The work at the Yard will take up all the winter. The amphitheatre will be open to the public on the fourteenth of May, to the day. The Easter holidays will fall a month earlier; and you shall marry my god-daughter during the holidays. Not a word; leave it to me. And leave both your settlements and your prospects to me as well. You can understand, my boy, that, when money is pouring in like water—as it will without a doubt—Victorien Beaugrand will throw up a profession which does not give him sufficient leisure for his private studies and that he will live with me, he and his wife. Yes, I said his wife; and I stick to it. Good-bye, my dear chap, not another word."

I walked on. He called me back:

"Say good-bye to me, Victorien."

He put his arms round me with greater fervour than usual; and I heard him murmur:

"Who can tell if we shall ever meet again? At my age! And threatened as I am, too!"

I protested. He embraced me yet again:

"You're right. I am really talking nonsense. You think of your

40

marriage. Bérangère is a dear, sweet girl. And she loves you. Good-bye and bless you! I'll write to you. Good-bye."

I confess that Noël Dorgeroux's ambitions, at least in so far as they related to the turning of his discovery to practical account, did not strike me as absurd; and what I have said of the things seen at the Yard will exempt me, I imagine, from stating the reasons for my confidence. For the moment, therefore, I will leave the question aside and say no more of those three haunting eyes or the phantasmal scenes upon the magic screen. But how could I indulge the dreams of the future which Noël Dorgeroux suggested? How could I forget Bérangère's hostile attitude, her ambiguous conduct?

True, during the months that followed, I often sought to cling to the delightful memory of the vision which I had surprised and the charming picture of Bérangère bending over me with that soft look in her eyes. But I very soon pulled myself up and cried:

"I saw the thing all wrong! What I took for affection and, God forgive me, for love was only the expression of a woman triumphing over a man's abasement! Bérangère does not care for me. The movement that threw her against my shoulder was due to a sort of nervous crisis; and she felt so much ashamed of it that she at once pushed me away and ran indoors. Besides, she had an appointment with that man the very next day and, in order to keep it, let me go without saying good-bye to me."

My months of exile therefore were painful months. I wrote to Bérangère in vain. I received no reply.

My uncle in his letters spoke of nothing but the Yard. The works were making quick progress. The amphitheatre was growing taller and taller. The wall was quite transformed. The last news, about the middle of March, told me that nothing remained to be done but to fix the thousand seats, which had long been on order, and to hang the iron curtain which was to protect the screen.

It was at this period that Noël Dorgeroux's misgivings revived, or at least it was then that he mentioned them when writing to me. Two books which he bought in Paris and which he used to read in private, lest his choice of a subject should enable anyone to learn the secret of his discovery, had been removed, taken away and then restored to their place. A sheet of paper, covered with notes and chemical formulae, disappeared. There were footprints in the garden. The writing-desk had been broken open, in the room where he worked at the Lodge since the demolition of the sheds.

This last incident, I confess, caused me a certain alarm. My uncle's fears were shown to be based upon a serious fact. There was evidently some one prowling around the Lodge and forcing an entrance in pursuance of a scheme whose nature was easy to guess.

Involuntarily I thought of the man with the glasses and his relations with Bérangère. There was no knowing. . . .

I made a fresh attempt to persuade the girl to communicate with me:

"You know what's happening at the Lodge, don't you?" I wrote. "How do you explain those facts, which to me seem pretty significant? Be sure to send me word if you feel the least uneasiness. And keep a close watch in the meantime."

I followed up this letter with two telegrams dispatched in quick succession. But Bérangère's stubborn silence, instead of distressing me, served rather to allay my apprehensions. She would not have failed to send for me had there been any danger. No, my uncle was mistaken. He was a victim to the feverish condition into which his discovery was throwing him. As the date approached on which he had decided to make it public, he felt anxious. But there was nothing to justify his apprehensions.

I allowed a few more days to elapse. Then I wrote Bérangère a letter of twenty pages, filled with reproaches, which I did not post. Her behaviour exasperated me. I suffered from a bitter fit of jealousy.

At last, on Saturday, the twenty-ninth of March, I received from my uncle a registered bundle of papers and a very explicit letter, which I kept and which I am copying verbatim:

"My Dear Victorien,

"Recent events, combined with certain very serious circumstances of which I will tell you, prove that I am the object of a cunningly devised plot against which I have perhaps delayed defending myself longer than I ought. At any rate, it is my duty, in the midst of the dangers which threaten my very life, to protect the magnificent discovery which mankind will owe to my efforts and to take precautionary measures which you will certainly not think unwarranted.

"I have, therefore, drawn up—as I always refused to do before—a detailed report of my discovery, the investigations that led up to it and the conclusions to which my experiments have led me. However improbable it may seem, however contrary to all the accepted laws, the truth is as I state and not otherwise.

"I have added to my report a very exact definition of the technical processes which should be employed in the installation and exploitation of my discovery, as also of my special views upon the financial management of the amphitheatre, the advertising, the floating of the business and the manner in which it might subsequently be extended by building in the garden and where the Lodge now stands a second amphitheatre to face the other side of the wall.

"I am sending you this report by the same post, sealed and registered, and I will ask you not to open it unless I come by some harm. As an additional precaution, I have not included in it the chemical formula which has resulted from my labours and which is the actual basis of my discovery. You will find it engraved on a small and very thin steel plate which I always carry inside the lining of my waistcoat. In this way you and you alone will have in your hands all the necessary factors for exploiting the invention. This will need no special qualifications or scientific preparation. The report and the formula are ample. Holding these two, you are master of the situation; and no one can ever rob you of the material profits of the wonderful secret which I am bequeathing to you.

"And now, my dear boy, let us hope that all my presentiments are unfounded and that we shall soon be celebrating together the happy events which I foresee, including first and foremost your marriage with Bérangère. I have not yet been able to obtain a favourable reply from her and she has for some time appeared to me to be, as you put it, in a rather fanciful mood; but I have no doubt that your return will make her reconsider a refusal which she does not even attempt to justify.

"Ever affectionately yours,

Noël Dorgeroux."

This letter reached me too late to allow me to catch the evening express. Besides, was there any urgency for my departure? Ought I not to wait for further news?

A casual observation made short work of my hesitation. As I sat reflecting, mechanically turning the envelope in my hands, I perceived that it had been opened and then fastened down again; what is more, this had been done rather clumsily, probably by some one who had only a few seconds at his disposal.

The full gravity of the situation at once flashed across my mind. The man who had opened the letter before it was dispatched and who beyond a doubt was the man whom Noël Dorgeroux accused of plotting, this man now knew that Noël Dorgeroux carried on his person, in the lining of his waistcoat, a steel plate bearing an inscription containing the essential formula.

I examined the registered packet and observed that it had not been opened. Nevertheless, at all costs, though I was firmly resolved not to read my uncle's report, I undid the string and discovered a pasteboard tube. Inside this tube was a roll of paper which I eagerly examined. It consisted of blank pages and nothing else. The report had been stolen.

Three hours later, I was seated in a night train which did not reach Paris until the afternoon of the next day, Sunday. It was four o'clock when I walked out of the station at Meudon. The enemy had for at least two days known the contents of my uncle's letter, his report and the dreadful means of procuring the formula.

CHAPTER VII

THE FIERCE-EYED MAN

The staff at the Lodge consisted in its entirety of one old maid-servant, a little deaf and very short-sighted, who combined the functions, as occasion demanded, of parlour-maid, cook and gardener. Notwithstanding these manifold duties, Valentine hardly ever left her kitchen-range, which was situated in an extension built on to the house and opening directly upon the street.

This was where I found her. She did not seem surprised at my return—nothing, for that matter, ever surprised or perturbed her—and I at once saw that she was still living outside the course of events and that she would be unable to tell me anything useful. I gathered, however, that my uncle and Bérangère had gone out half an hour earlier.

"Together?" I asked.

"Good gracious, no! The master came through the kitchen and said, 'I'm going to post a letter. Then I shall go to the Yard.' He left a bottle behind him, you know, one of those blue medicine-bottles which he uses for his experiments."

"Where did he leave it, Valentine?"

"Why, over there, on the dresser. He must have forgotten it when he put on his overcoat, for he never parts with those bottles of his."

"It's not there, Valentine."

"Now that's a funny thing! M. Dorgeroux hasn't been back, I know."

"And has no one else been?"

"No. Yes, there has, though; a gentleman, a gentleman who came for Mlle. Bérangère a little while after."

"And did you go to fetch her?"

"Yes."

"Then it must have been while you were away ..."

"You don't mean that! Oh, how M. Dorgeroux will scold me!"

"But who is the gentleman?"

"Upon my word, I couldn't tell you.... My sight is so bad...."

"Do you know him?"

"No, I didn't recognize his voice."

"And did they both go out, Bérangère and he?"

"Yes, they crossed the road ... opposite."

Opposite meant the path in the wood.

I thought for a second or two; and then, tearing a sheet of paper from my note-book, I wrote:

"My Dear Uncle,

"Wait for me, when you come back, and don't leave the Lodge on any account. The danger is imminent.

"Victorien."

"Give this to M. Dorgeroux as soon as you see him, Valentine. I shall be back in half an hour."

The path ran in a straight line through dense thickets with tiny leaves burgeoning on the twigs of the bushes. It had rained heavily during the last few days, but a bright spring sun was drying the ground and I could distinguish no trace of footsteps. After walking three hundred yards, however, I met a small boy of the neighbourhood, whom I knew by sight, coming back to the village and pushing his bicycle, which had burst a tyre.

"You don't happen to have seen Mlle. Bérangère, have you?" I asked.

"Yes," he said, "with a gentleman."

"A gentleman wearing glasses?"

"Yes, a tall chap, with a big beard."

"Are they far away?"

"When I saw them, they were a mile and a quarter from here. I turned back later ... they had taken the old road ... the one that goes to the left."

I quickened my pace, greatly excited, for I was conscious of an increasing dread. I reached the old road. But, a little farther on, it brought me to an open space crossed by a number of paths. Which was I to take?

Feeling more and more anxious, I called out:

"Bérangère! ... Bérangère!"

Presently I heard the hum of an engine and the sound of a motor-car getting under way. It must have been five hundred yards from where I was. I turned down a path in which, almost at once, I saw footsteps very clearly marked in the mud, the footsteps of a man and of a woman. These led me to the entrance of a cemetery which had not been used for over twenty years and which, standing on the boundary of two parishes, had become the subject of claims, counterclaims and litigation generally.

I made my way in. The tall grass had been trampled down along two lines which skirted the wall, passed before the remnants of what had once been the keeper's cottage, joined around the kerb of a cistern fitted up as a well and were next continued to the wall of a half-demolished little mortuary chapel.

Between the cistern and the chapel the soil had been trodden several times over. Beyond the chapel there was only one track of footsteps, those of a man.

I confess that just then my legs gave way beneath me, although there was no trace of a definite idea in my mind. I examined the inside of the chapel and then walked round it.

Something lying on the ground, at the foot of the only wall that was left wholly standing, attracted my attention. It was a number of bits of loose plaster which had fallen there and which were of a dark-grey colour that at once reminded me of the sort of wash with which the screen in the Yard was coated.

I looked up. More pieces of plaster of the same colour, placed flat against the wall and held in position by clamp-headed nails, formed another screen, an incomplete, broken screen, on which I could plainly see that a quite fresh layer of substance had been spread.

By whom? Evidently by one of the two persons whom I was tracking, by the man with the eye-glasses or by Bérangère, perhaps even by both. But with what object? Was it to conjure up the miraculous vision? And was I to believe—the supposition really forced itself upon me as a certainty—that the fragments of plaster had first been stolen from the rubbish in the Yard and then pieced together like a mosaic?

In that case, if the conditions were the same, if the necessary substance was spread precisely in accordance with the details of the discovery, if I was standing opposite a screen identical at all points with the other, it was possible ... it was possible. . . .

While this question was taking shape, my mind received so plain an answer that I saw the Three Eyes before they emerged from the depths whence I was waiting for them to appear. The image which I was evoking blended gradually with the real image which was forming and which presently opened its threefold gaze upon me, a fixed and gloomy gaze.

Here, then, as yonder, in the abandoned cemetery as in the Yard where Noël Dorgeroux summoned his inexplicable phantoms from the void, the Three Eyes were awakening to life. Chipped in one place, cracked in another, they looked through the fragments of disjointed plaster as they had done through the carefully tended screen. They gazed in this solitude just as though Noël Dorgeroux had been there to kindle and feed their mysterious flame.

The gloomy eyes, however, were changing their expression. They became wicked, cruel, implacable, ferocious even. Then they faded away; and I waited for the spectacle which those three geometrical figures generally heralded. And in fact, after a break, there was a sort of pulsating light, but so confused that it was difficult for me to make out any clearly defined scenes.

I could barely distinguish some trees, a river with an eyot in it, a low-roofed house and some people; but all this was vague, misty, unfinished, broken up by the cracks in the screen, impeded by causes of which I was ignorant. One might have fancied a certain hesitation in the will that evoked the image. Moreover, after a few fruitless attempts and an effort of which I perceived the futility, the image abruptly faded away and everything relapsed into death and emptiness.

"Death and emptiness," I said aloud.

I repeated the words several times over. They rang within me like a funereal echo with which the memory of Bérangère was mingled. The nightmare of the Three Eyes became one with the nightmare that drove me in pursuit of her. And I remained standing in front of the gruesome chapel, uncertain, not knowing what to do.

Bérangère's footprints brought me back to the well, near which I found in four places the marks of both her slender soles and both her pointed heels. The well was covered with a small, tiled dome. Formerly a bucket was lowered by means of a pulley to bring up the rainwater that had been gathered from the roof of the house.

There was of course no valid reason to make me believe that a crime had been committed. The footmarks did not constitute a sufficient clue. Nevertheless I felt myself bathed in perspiration; and, leaning over the open mouth, from which floated a damp and mildewed breath I faltered:

"Bérangère!"

I heard not a sound.

I lit a piece of paper, which I screwed into a torch, throwing a glimmer of light into the widened reservoir of the cistern. But I saw nothing save a sheet of water, black as ink and motionless.

"No," I protested, "it's impossible. I have no right to imagine such an atrocity. Why should they have killed her? It was my uncle who was threatened, not she."

At all events I continued my search and followed the man's single track. This led me to the far side of the cemetery and then to an avenue of fir-trees, where I came upon some cans of petrol. The motor-car had started from here. The tracks of the tyres ran through the wood.

I went no farther. It suddenly occurred to me that I ought before all to think of my uncle, to defend him and to take joint measures with him.

I therefore turned in the direction of the post-office. But, remembering that this was Sunday and that my uncle after dropping his letter in the box, had certainly gone back to the Yard, I ran to the Lodge and called out to Valentine:

"Has my uncle come in? Has he had my note?"

"No, no," she said. "I told you, the master has gone to the Yard."

"Exactly: he must have come this way!"

"Not at all. Coming from the post-office, he would go straight through the new entrance to the amphitheatre."

"In that case," I said, "all I need do is to go through the garden."

I hurried away, but the little door was locked. And from that moment, though there was nothing to prove my uncle's presence in the Yard, I felt certain that he was there and also felt afraid that my assistance had come too late.

I called. No one answered. The door remained shut.

Then, terrified, I went back to the house and out into the street and ran round the premises on the left, in order to go in by the new entrance.

This turned out to be a tall gate, flanked on either side by a ticket-office and giving access to a large courtyard, in which stood the back of the amphitheatre.

This gate also was closed, by means of a strong chain which my uncle had padlocked behind him.

What was I to do? Remembering how Bérangère and then I myself had climbed over the wall one day, I followed the other side of the Yard, in order to reach the old lamp-post. The same deserted path skirted the same stout plank fence, the corner of which ran into the fields.

When I came to this corner, I saw the lamp-post. At that moment, a man appeared on the top of the wall, caught hold of the post and let himself down by it. There was no room for doubt; the man leaving the Yard in this way had just been with my uncle. What had passed between them?

The distance that separated us was too great to allow me to distinguish his features. As soon as he saw me, he turned down the brim of his soft hat and drew the two ends of a muffler over his face. A loose-fitting grey rain-coat concealed his figure. I received the impression, however, that he was shorter and thinner than the man with the eye-glasses.

"Stop!" I cried, as he moved away.

My summons only hastened his flight; and it was in vain that I darted forward in his pursuit, shouting insults at him and threatening him with a revolver which I did not possess. He covered the whole width of the fields, leapt over a hedge and reached the skirt of the woods.

I was certainly younger than he, for I soon perceived that the interval between us was decreasing; and I should have caught him up, if we had been running across open country. But I lost sight of him at the first clump of trees; and I was nearly abandoning the attempt to come up with him, when, suddenly, he retraced his steps and seemed to be looking for something.

I made a rush for him. He did not appear to be perturbed by my approach. He merely drew a revolver and pointed it at me, without saying a word or ceasing his investigations.

I now saw what his object was. Something lay gleaming in the grass. It was a piece of metal which, I soon perceived, was none other than the steel plate on which Noël Dorgeroux had engraved the chemical formula.

We both flung ourselves on the ground at the same time. I was the first to seize the strip of steel. But a hand gripped mine; and on this hand, which was half-covered by the sleeve of the rain-coat, there was blood.

I was startled and suffered from a moment's faintness. The vision of Noël Dorgeroux dying, nay, dead, had flashed upon me so suddenly that the man succeeded in overpowering me and stretching me underneath him.

As we thus lay one against the other, with our faces almost touching, I saw only part of his, the lower half being hidden by the muffler. But his two eyes glared at me, under the shadow of his hat; and we stared at each other in silence, while our hands continued to grapple.

Those eyes of his were cruel and implacable, the eyes of a murderer whose whole being is bent upon the supreme effort of killing. Where had I seen them before? For I certainly knew those fiercely glittering eyes. Their gaze penetrated my brain at a spot into which it had already been deeply impressed. It bore a familiar look, a look which had crossed my own before. But when? In what eyes had I seen that expression? In the eyes looming out of the wall perhaps? The eyes shown on the fabulous screen?

Yes, yes, those were the eyes! I recognized them now! They had shone in the infinite space that lay in the depths of the plaster! They had lived before my sight, a few minutes ago, on the ruined wall of the mortuary chapel. They were the same cruel, pitiless eyes, the eyes which had perturbed me then even as they were perturbing me now, sapping my last remnant of strength.

I released my hold. The man sprang up, caught me a blow on

the forehead with the butt of his revolver and ran away, carrying the steel plate with him.

This time I did not think of pursuing him. Without doing me any great hurt, the blow which I received had stunned me. I was still tottering on my feet when I heard, in the woods, the same sound of an engine being started and a car getting under way which I had heard near the cemetery. The motor-car, driven by the man with the eye-glasses, had come to fetch my assailant. The two confederates, after having probably rid themselves of Bérangère and certainly rid themselves of Noël Dorgeroux, were making off. . . .

My heart wrung with anguish, I hurried back to the foot of the old lamp-post, hoisted myself to the top of the fence and in this way jumped into the front part of the Yard, contained between the main wall and the new structure of the amphitheatre.

This wall, entirely rebuilt, taller and wider than it used to be, now had the size and the importance of the outer wall of a Greek or Roman amphitheatre. Two square columns and a canopy marked the place of the screen, whose plaster, from the distance at which I stood, did not seem yet to be coated with its layer of a dark-grey composition, which explained why my uncle had left it uncovered. Nor could I at first see the lower part, which was concealed by a heap of materials of all kinds. But how certain I felt of what I should see when I came nearer! How well I knew what was there, behind those planks and building-stones!

My legs were trembling. I had to seek a support. It cost me an untold effort to take a few steps forward.

Right against the wall, in the very middle of his Yard, Noël Dorgeroux lay prone, his arms twisted beneath him.

A cursory inspection showed me that he had been murdered with a pick-axe.

CHAPTER VIII

"SOME ONE WILL EMERGE
FROM THE DARKNESS"

Notwithstanding Noël Dorgeroux's advanced age, there had been a violent struggle. The murderer, whose footprints I traced along the path which led from the fence to the wall, had flung himself upon his victim and had first tried to strangle him. It was not until later, in the second phase of the contest, that he had seized a pick-axe with which to strike Noël Dorgeroux.

Nothing of intrinsic value had been stolen. I found my uncle's watch and note-case untouched. But the waistcoat had been opened; and the lining, which formed a pocket, was, of course, empty.

For the moment I wasted no time in the Yard. Passing through the garden and the Lodge, where I told old Valentine in a few words what had happened, I called the nearest neighbours, sent a boy running to the mayor's and went on to the disused cemetery, accompanied by some men with ropes, a ladder and a lantern. It was growing dark when we arrived.

I had decided to go down the cistern myself; and I did so without experiencing any great emotion. Notwithstanding the reasons which led me to fear that Bérangère might have been thrown into it, the crime appeared to me to be absolutely improbable. And I was right. Nevertheless, at the bottom of the cistern, which was perforated by obvious cracks and held only a few puddles of stagnant water, I picked up in the mud, among the stones, brickbats and potsherds, an empty bottle, the neck of which had been knocked off. I was struck by its blue colour. This was doubtless the bottle which had been taken from the dresser at the Lodge. Besides, when I brought it back to the Lodge that evening, Valentine identified it for certain.

What had happened might therefore be reconstructed as follows: the man with the eye-glasses, having the bottle in his possession, had gone to the cemetery to meet the motor-car which was waiting for him and had stopped in front of the chapel, to which were nailed the fragments from the old wall in the Yard. These fragments he had smeared with the liquid contained in the bottle. Then, when he heard me coming, he threw the bottle down the well and, without having time to see the picture which I myself was to see ten minutes later, he ran away and went off in the car to pick up Noël Dorgeroux's murderer near the Yard.

Things as they turned out confirmed my explanation, or at least confirmed it to a great extent. But what of Bérangère? What part had she played in all this? And where was she now?

The enquiry, first instituted in the Yard by the local police, was pursued next day by a magistrate and two detectives, assisted by myself. We learnt that the car containing the two accomplices had come from Paris on the morning of the day before and that it had returned to Paris the same night. Both coming and going it had carried two men whose descriptions tallied exactly with that of the two criminals.

We were favoured by an extraordinary piece of luck. A road-mender working near the ornamental water in the Bois de Boulogne told us, when we asked him about the motor-car, that he recognized it as having been garaged in a coach-house close by the house in which he lived and that he recognized the man with the eye-glasses as one of the tenants of this same house!

He gave us the address. The house was behind the Jardin des Batignolles. It was an old barrack of a tenement-house swarming with tenants. As soon as we had described to the concierge the person for whom we were searching, she exclaimed:

"You mean M. Velmot, a tall, good-looking man, don't you? He has had a furnished flat here for over six months, but he only sleeps here now and again. He is out of town a great deal."

"Did he sleep at home last night?"

"Yes. He came back yesterday evening, in his motor, with a gentleman whom I had never seen before; and they did not leave until this morning."

"In the motor?"

"No. The car is in the garage."

"Have you the key of the flat?"

"Of course! I do the housework!"

"Show us over, please."

The flat consisted of three small rooms; a dining-room and two bedrooms. It contained no clothes or papers. M. Velmot had taken everything with him in a portmanteau, as he did each time he went away, said the concierge. But pinned to the wall, amid a number of sketches, was a drawing which represented the Three Eyes so faithfully that it could not have been made except by some one who had seen the miraculous visions.

"Let's go to the garage," said one of the detectives.

We had to call in a locksmith to gain admittance. In addition to the muffler and a coat stained with blood we found two more mufflers and three silk handkerchiefs, all twisted and spoilt. The identification-plate of the car had been recently unscrewed. The number, newly repainted, must be false. Apart from these details there was nothing specially worth noting.

I am trying to sum up the phases of the preliminary and magisterial enquiries as briefly as possible. This narrative is not a detective-story any more than a love-story. The riddle of the Three Eyes, together with its solution, forms the only object of these pages and the only interest which the reader can hope to find in them. But, at the stage which we have reached, it is easy to understand that all these events were so closely interwoven that it is impossible to separate one from the other. One detail governs the next, which in its turn affects what came before.

So I must repeat my earlier question: what part was Bérangère playing in it all? And what had become of her? She had disappeared, suddenly, somewhere near the chapel. Beyond that point there was not a trace of her, not a clue. And this inexplicable disappearance marked the conclusion of several successive weeks during which, we are bound to admit, the girl's behaviour might easily seem odd to the most indulgent eyes.

I felt this so clearly that I declared, emphatically, in the course of my evidence:

"She was caught in a trap and carried off."

"Prove it," they retorted. "Find some justification for the appointments which she made and kept all through the winter with the fellow whom you call the man with the glasses, in other words, with the man Velmot."

And the police based their suspicions on a really disturbing charge which they had discovered and which had escaped me. During his struggle with his assailant, very likely at the moment when the latter, after reducing him to a state of helplessness, had moved away to fetch the pick-axe, Noël Dorgeroux had managed to scrawl a few words with a broken flint at the foot of the screen. The writing was very faint and almost illegible, for the flint in places had merely scratched the plaster; nevertheless, it was possible to decipher the following:

"B-ray.... Berge..."

The term "B-ray" evidently referred to Noël Dorgeroux's invention. My uncle's first thought, when threatened with death, had been to convey in the briefest (but, unfortunately, also the most unintelligible) form the particulars which would save his marvellous discovery from oblivion. "B-ray" was an expression which he himself understood but which suggested nothing to those who did not know what he meant by it.

The five letters "B.E.R.G.E.," on the other hand, allowed of only one interpretation. "Berge" stood for Bergeronnette, the pet name by which Noël Dorgeroux called his god-daughter.

"Very well," I exclaimed before the magistrate, who had taken me to the screen. "Very well, I agree with your interpretation. It relates to Bérangère. But my uncle was simply wishing to express his love for her and his extreme anxiety on her behalf. In writing his god-daughter's name at the very moment when he is in mortal danger, he shows that he is uneasy about her, that he is recommending her to our care."

"Or that he is accusing her," retorted the magistrate.

Bérangère accused by my uncle! Bérangère capable of sharing in the murder of her god-father! I remember shrugging my shoulders. But there was no reply that I could make beyond protests based upon no actual fact and contradicted by appearances.

All that I said was:

"I fail to see what interest she could have had! ..."

"A very considerable interest: the exploitation of the wonderful secret which you have mentioned."

"But she is ignorant of the secret!"

"How do you know? She's not ignorant of it, if she is in league with the two accomplices. The manuscript which M. Dorgeroux sent you has disappeared: who was in a better position than she to steal it? However, mark me, I make no assertions. I have my suspicions, that's all; and I'm trying to discover what I can."

But the most minute investigations led to no result. Was Bérangère also a victim of the two criminals?

Her father was written to, at Toulouse. The man Massignac replied that he had been in bed for a fortnight with a sharp attack of influenza, that he would come to Paris as soon as he was well, but that, having had no news of his daughter for years, he was unable to furnish any particulars about her.

So, when all was said and done, whether kidnapped, as I preferred to believe, or in hiding, as the police suspected, Bérangère was nowhere to be found.

Meanwhile, the public was beginning to grow excited about a case which, before long, was to rouse it to a pitch of delirium. No doubt at first there was merely a question of the crime itself. The murder of Noël Dorgeroux, the abduction of his god-daughter—the police consented, at my earnest entreaties, to accept this as the official version—the theft of my uncle's manuscript, the theft of the formula: all this, at the outset, only puzzled men's minds as a cunningly-devised conspiracy and a cleverly-executed crime. But not many days elapsed before the revelations which I was constrained to make diverted all the attention of the newspapers and all the curiosity of the public to Noël Dorgeroux's discovery.

For I had to speak, notwithstanding the promise of silence which I had given my uncle. I had to answer the magistrate's questions, to tell all I knew, to explain matters, to enter into details, to write a report, to protest against ill-formed judgments, to rectify mistakes, to specify, enumerate, classify, in short, to confide to the authorities and incidentally to the eager reporters all that my uncle had said to me, all his dreams, all the wonders of the Yard, all the phantasmal visions which I had beheld upon the screen.

Before a week was over, Paris, France, the whole world knew in every detail, save for the points which concerned Bérangère and myself alone, what was at once and spontaneously described as the mystery of the Three Eyes.

Of course I was met with irony, sarcasm and uproarious laughter. A miracle finds no believers except among its astounded witnesses. And what but a miracle could be put forward as the cause of a phenomenon which, I maintained, had no credible cause? The execution of Edith Cavell was a miracle. So was the representation of the fight between two airmen. So was the scene in which Noël Dorgeroux's son was hit by a bullet. So, above all, was the looming of those Three Eyes, which throbbed with life, which gazed at the spectator and which were the eyes of the very people about to figure in the spectacle as the actors thus miraculously announced!

Nevertheless, one by one, voices were raised in my defence. My past was gone into, the value of my evidence was weighed; and, though people were still inclined to accuse me of being a visionary or a sick man, subject to hallucinations, at least they had to admit my absolute bona fides. A party of adherents took up the cudgels for me. There was a noisy battle of opinions. Ah, my poor uncle Dorgeroux had asked for wide publicity for his amphitheatre! His fondest wishes were far exceeded by the strident and tremendous clamour which continued like an unbroken peal of thunder.

For the rest, all this uproar was dominated by one idea, which took shape gradually and summed up the thousand theories which every one was indulging. I am copying it from a newspaper-article which I carefully preserved:

"In any case, whatever opinion we may hold of Noël Dorgeroux's alleged discovery, whatever view we may take of M. Victorien Beaugrand's common sense and mental equilibrium, one thing is certain, which is that we shall sooner or later know the truth. When two such competent people as Velmot and his accomplice join forces to accomplish a definite task, namely, the theft of a scientific secret, when they carry out their plot so skilfully, when they succeed beyond all hopes, their object, it will be agreed, is certainly not that they may enjoy the results of their enterprise by stealth.

"If they have Noël Dorgeroux's manuscript in their hands, together with the chemical formula that completes it, their intention beyond a doubt is to make all the profits on which Noël Dorgeroux himself was counting. To make these profits the secret must first be exploited. And, to exploit a secret of this kind, its possessors must act openly, publicly, in the face of the world. And, to do this, it will not pay them to settle down in a remote corner in France or elsewhere and to set up another enterprise. It will not pay, because, in any case, there would be the same confession of guilt. No, it will pay them better and do them no more harm to take up their quarters frankly and cynically in the amphitheatre of the Yard and to make use of what has there been accomplished, under the most promising conditions, by Noël Dorgeroux.

"To sum up, therefore. Before long, some one will emerge from the darkness. Some one will remove the mask from his face. The sequel and the conclusion of the unfinished plot will be enacted in their fullness. And, three weeks hence, on the date fixed, the 14th of May, we shall witness the inauguration of the amphitheatre erected by Noël Dorgeroux. And this inauguration will take place under the vigorous management of the man who will be, who already is, the owner of the secret: a formidable person, we must admit."

The argument was strictly logical. Stolen jewels are sold in secret. Money changes hands anonymously. But an invention yields no profit unless it is exploited.

Meanwhile the days passed and no one emerged from the darkness. The two accomplices betrayed not a sign of life. It was now known that Velmot, the man with the glasses, had practised all sorts of callings. Some Paris manufacturers, for whom he had travelled in the provinces, furnished an exact description of his person. The police learnt a number of things about him, but not enough to enable them to lay hands upon him.

Nor did a careful scrutiny of Noël Dorgeroux's papers supply the least information. All that the authorities found was a sealed, unaddressed envelope, which they opened. The contents surprised me greatly. They consisted of a will, dated five years back, in which Noël Dorgeroux, while naming me as his residuary legatee, gave and bequeathed to his god-daughter, Bérangère Massignac the piece of ground known as the Yard and everything that the Yard might contain on the day of his death. With the exception of this document, which was of no importance, since my uncle, in one of his last letters to me, had expressed different intentions, they found nothing but immaterial notes which had no bearing upon the great secret. Thereupon they indulged in the wildest conjectures and wandered about in a darkness which not even the sworn chemists called in to examine the screen were able to dispel. The wall revealed nothing in particular, for the layer of plaster with which it was covered had not received the special glaze; and it was precisely the formula of this glaze that constituted Noël Dorgeroux's secret.

But the glaze existed on the old chapel in the cemetery, where I had seen the geometrical figure of the Three Eyes appear. Yes, they certainly found something clinging to the surface of the fragments of plaster taken from that spot. But they were not able with this something to produce a compound capable of yielding any sort of vision. The right formula was obviously lacking; and so, no doubt, was some essential ingredient which had already been eliminated by the sun or the rain.

At the end of April there was no reason to believe in the prophecies which announced a theatrical culmination as inevitable. And the curiosity of the public increased at each fresh disappointment and on each new day spent in waiting. Noël Dorgeroux's yard had become a place of pilgrimage. Motor-cars and carriages arrived in swarms. The people crowded outside the locked gates and the fence, trying to catch a glimpse of the wall. I even received letters containing offers to buy the Yard at any price that I chose to name.

One day, old Valentine showed into the drawing-room a gentleman who said that he had come on important business. I saw a man of medium height with hair which was turning grey and with a face which was wider than it was long and which was made still wider by a pair of bushy whiskers and a perpetual smile. His threadbare dress and down-at-heel shoes denoted anything but a brilliant financial position. He expressed himself at once, however, in the language of a person to whom money is no object:

"I have any amount of capital behind me," he declared, cheerfully and before he had even told me his name. "My plans are made. All that remains is for you and me to come to terms."

"What on?" I asked.

"Why, on the business that I have come to propose to you!"

"I am sorry, sir," I replied, "but I am doing no business."

"That's a pity!" he cried, still more cheerfully and with his mouth spreading still farther across his face. "That's a pity! I should have been glad to take you into partnership. However, since you're not willing, I shall act alone, without of course exceeding the rights which I have in the Yard."

"Your rights in the Yard?" I echoed, astounded at his assurance.

"Why, rather!" he answered, with a loud laugh. "My rights: that's the only word."

"I don't follow you."

"I admit that it's not very clear. Well, suppose—you'll soon understand—suppose that I have come into Noël Dorgeroux's property."

I was beginning to lose patience and I took the fellow up sharply:

"I have no time to spare for jesting, sir. Noël Dorgeroux left no relatives except myself."

"I didn't say that I had come into his property as a relative."

"As what, then?"

"As an heir, simply ... as the lawful heir, specifically named as such by Noël Dorgeroux."

I was a little taken aback and, after a moment's thought, rejoined:

"Do you mean to say that Noël Dorgeroux made a will in your favour?"

"I do."

"Show it to me."

"There's no need to show it to you: you've seen it."

"I've seen it?"

"You saw it the other day. It must be in the hands of the examining-magistrate or the solicitor."

I lost my temper:

"Oh, it's that you're speaking of! Well, to begin with, the will isn't valid. I have a letter from my uncle ..."

He interrupted me:

"That letter doesn't affect the validity of the will. Any one will tell you that."

"And then?" I exclaimed. "Granting that it is valid, Noël Dorgeroux mentions nobody in it except myself for the Lodge and his god-daughter for the Yard. The only one who benefits, except myself, is Bérangère."

"Quite so, quite so," replied the man, without changing countenance. "But nobody knows what has become of Bérangère Massignac. Suppose that she were dead ..."

I grew indignant:

"She's not dead! It's quite impossible that she should be dead!"

"Very well," he said, calmly. "Then suppose that she's alive, that she's been kidnapped or that she's in hiding. In any event, one fact is certain, which is that she is under twenty, consequently she's a minor and consequently she cannot administer her own property. From the legal point of view she exists only in the person of her natural representative, her guardian, who in this case happens to be her father."

"And her father?" I asked, anxiously.

"Is myself."

He put on his hat, took it off again with a bow and said:

"Théodore Massignac, forty-two years of age, a native of Toulouse, a commercial traveller in wines."

It was a violent blow. The truth suddenly appeared to me in all its brutal nakedness. This man, this shady and wily individual, was Bérangère's father; and he had come in the name of the two accomplices, working in their interest and placing at their service the powers with which circumstances had favoured him.

"Her father?" I murmured. "Can it be possible? Are you her father?"

"Why, yes," he replied, with a fresh outburst of hilarity, "I'm the girl's daddy and, as such, the beneficiary, with the right to draw the profits for the next eighteen months, of Noël Dorgeroux's bequest. For eighteen months only! You can imagine that I'm itching to take possession of the estate, to complete the works and to prepare for the fourteenth of May an inauguration worthy in every respect of my old friend Dorgeroux."

I felt the beads of perspiration trickling down my forehead. He had spoken the words which were expected and foretold. He was the man of whom public opinion had said:

"When the time comes, some one will emerge from the darkness."

CHAPTER IX

THE MAN WHO EMERGED
FROM THE DARKNESS

"When the time comes," they had said, "some one will emerge from the darkness. When the time comes, some one will remove the mask from his face."

That face now beamed expansively before me. That some one, who was about to play the game of the two accomplices, was Bérangère's father. And the same question continued to suggest itself, each time more painfully than the last:

"What had been Bérangère's part in the horrible tragedy?"

There was a long, heavy silence between us. I began to stride across the room and stopped near the chimney, where a dying fire was smouldering. Thence I could see Massignac in a mirror, without his perceiving it; and his face, in repose, surprised me by a gloomy expression which was not unknown to me. I had probably seen some photograph of him in Bérangère's possession.

"It's curious," I said, "that your daughter should not have written to you."

I had turned round very briskly; nevertheless he had had time to expand his mouth and to resume his smile:

"Alas," he said, "the dear child hardly ever wrote to me and cared little about her poor daddy. I, on the other hand, am very fond of her. A daughter's always a daughter, you know. So you can imagine how I jumped for joy when I read in the papers that she had come into money. I should at last be able to devote myself to her and to devote all my strength and all my energy to the great and wonderful task of defending her interests and her fortune."

He spoke in a honeyed voice and assumed a false and unctuous air which exasperated me. I questioned him:

"How do you propose to fulfill that task?"

"Why, quite simply," he replied, "by continuing Noël Dorgeroux's work."

"In other words?"

"By throwing open the doors of the amphitheatre."

"Which means?"

"Which means that I shall show to the public the pictures which your uncle used to produce."

"Have you ever seen them?"

"No. I speak from your evidence and your interviews."

61

"Do you know how my uncle used to produce them?"

"I do, since yesterday evening."

"Then you have seen the manuscript of which I was robbed and the formula stolen by the murderer?"

"Since yesterday evening, I say."

"But how?" I exclaimed, excitedly.

"How? By a simple trick."

"What do you mean?"

He showed me a bundle of newspapers of the day before and continued, with a smirking air:

"If you had read yesterday's newspapers, or at least the more important of them, carefully, you would have noticed a discreet advertisement in the special column. It read, 'Proprietor of the Yard wishes to purchase the two documents necessary for working. He can be seen this evening in the Place Vendôme.' Nothing much in the advertisement, was there? But, to the possessors of the two documents, how clear in its meaning ... and what a bait! To them it was the one opportunity of making a profit, for, with all the publicity attaching to the affair, they were unable to benefit by the result of their robberies without revealing their identity to the public. My calculation was correct. After I had waited an hour by the Vendôme Column, a very luxurious motor-car picked me up, you might almost say without stopping, and, ten minutes afterwards, dropped me at the Étoile, with the documents in my possession. I spent the night in reading the manuscript. Oh, my dear sir, what a genius your uncle was! What a revolution his discovery! And in what a masterly way he expounded it! I never read anything so methodical and so lucid! All that remains for me to do is mere child's-play."

I had listened to the man Massignac with ever-increasing amazement. Was he assuming that anybody would for a moment credit so ridiculous a tale?

He was laughing, however, with a look of a man who congratulates himself on the events with which he is mixed up, or rather, perhaps, on the very skilful fashion in which he believes himself to have manipulated them.

With one hand, I pushed in his direction the hat which he had laid on the table. Then I opened the door leading into the hall.

He rose and said:

"I am staying close by, at the Station Hotel. Would you mind having any letters sent there which may come for me here? For I suppose you have no room for me at the Lodge?"

I abruptly gripped him by the arm and cried:

"You know what you're risking, don't you?"

62

"In doing what?"

"In pursuing your enterprise."

"Upon my word, I don't quite see ..."

"Prison, sir, prison."

"Oh, come! Prison!"

"Prison, sir. The police will never accept all your stories and all your lies!"

His mouth widened into a new laugh:

"What big words! And how unjust, when addressed to a respectable father who seeks nothing but his daughter's happiness! No, no, sir, believe me, the inauguration will take place on the fourteenth of May ... unless, indeed, you oppose the wishes which your uncle expresses in his will...."

He gave me a questioning look, which betrayed a certain uneasiness; and I myself wavered as to the answer which I ought to give him. My hesitation yielded to a motive of which I did not weigh the value clearly but which seemed to me so imperious that I declared:

"I shall raise no opposition: not that I respect a will which does not represent my uncle's real intentions, but because I am bound to sacrifice everything to his fame. If Noël Dorgeroux's discovery depends on you, go ahead: the means which you have employed to get hold of it do not concern me."

With a fresh burst of merry laughter and a low bow, the fellow left the room. That evening, in the course of a visit to the solicitor, and next day, through the newspapers, he boldly set forth his claims, which, I may say, from the legal point of view, were recognized as absolutely legitimate. But, two days later, he was summoned to appear before the examining-magistrate and an enquiry was opened against him.

Against him is the right term. Certainly, there was no fact to be laid to his charge. Certainly, he was able to prove that he had been ill in bed, nursed by a woman-of-all-work who had been looking after him for a month, and that he had left his place in Toulouse only to come straight to Paris. But what had he done in Paris? Whom had he seen? From whom had he obtained the manuscript and the formula? He was unable to furnish explanations in reply to any of these questions.

He did not even try:

"I am pledged to secrecy," he said. "I gave my word of honour not to say anything about those who handed me the documents I needed."

The man Massignac's word of Honour! The man Massignac's scruples! Lies, of course! Hypocrisy! Subterfuge! But, all the same, however suspect the fellow might be, it was difficult to know of what to accuse him or how to sustain the accusation when made.

And then there was this element of strangeness, that the suspicion, the presumption, the certainty that the man Massignac was the willing tool of the two criminals, all this was swept away by the great movement of curiosity that carried people off their feet. Judicial procedure, ordinary precautions, regular adjournments, legal procrastinations which delay the entry into possession of the legatees were one and all neglected. The public wanted to see and know; and Théodore Massignac was the man who held the prodigious secret.

He was therefore allowed to have the keys of the amphitheatre and went in alone, or with labourers upon whom he kept an eye, replacing them by fresh gangs so as to avoid plots and machinations. He often went to Paris, throwing off the scent of the detectives who dogged his movements, and returned with bottles and cans carefully wrapped up.

On the day before that fixed for the inauguration, the police were no wiser than on the first day in matters concerning the man Massignac, or Velmot's hiding-place, or the murderer's, or Bérangère's. The same ignorance prevailed regarding Noël Dorgeroux's secret, the circumstances of his death and the ambiguous words which he had scribbled on the plaster of the wall. As for the miraculous visions which I have described, they were denied or accepted as vigorously and as unreasonably by both the disputing parties. In short, nobody knew anything.

And this perhaps was the reason why the thousand seats in the amphitheatre were sold out within a few hours. Priced at a hundred francs apiece, they were bought up by half-a-dozen speculators who got rid of them at two or three times their original cost. How delighted my poor uncle would have been had he lived to see it!

The night before the fourteenth of May, I slept very badly, haunted by nightmares that kept on waking me with a start. At the first glimmer of dawn, I was sitting on the side of my bed when, in the deep silence, which was barely broken by the twittering of a few birds, I seemed to hear the sound of a key in a lock and a door creaking on its hinges.

I must explain that, since my uncle's death, I had been sleeping next to the room that used to be his. Now the noise came from that room, from which I was separated only by a glazed door covered with a chintz curtain. I listened and heard the sound of a chair moved from its place. There was certainly some one in the next room; and this some one, obviously unaware that I occupied the adjoining chamber, was taking scarcely any precautions. But how had he got in?

I sprang from the bed, slipped on my trousers, took up a revolver and drew aside a corner of the curtain. At first, the shutters were closed and the room in darkness and I saw only an indistinct shadow. Then the window was opened softly. Somebody lifted the iron bar and pushed back the shutters, thus admitting the light.

I now saw a woman return to the middle of the room. She was draped from head to foot in a brown stuff cloak. Nevertheless I knew her at once. It was Bérangère.

I had a feeling not so much of amazement as of sudden and profound pity at the sight of her emaciated face, her poor face, once so bright and eager, now so sad and wan. I did not even think of rejoicing at the fact of her being alive, nor did I ask myself what clandestine business had brought her back to the Lodge. The one thing that held me captive was the painful spectacle of her pallid face, with its feverish, burning eyes and blue eyelids. Her cloak betrayed the shrunken figure beneath it.

Her heart must have been beating terribly, for she held her two hands to her breast to suppress its throbbing. She even had to lean on the edge of the table. She staggered and nearly fell. Poor Bérangère. I felt anguish-stricken as I watched her.

She pulled herself together, however, and looked around her. Then, with a tottering gait, she went to the mantelpiece, where two old engravings, framed in black with a gold beading, hung one on either side of the looking-glass. She climbed on a chair and took down the one on the right, a portrait of D'Alembert.

Stepping down from the chair, she examined the back of the frame, which was closed by a piece of old card-board the edges of which were fastened to the sides of the frame by strips of gummed cloth. Bérangère cut these strips with a pen-knife, bending back the tacks which held the cardboard in position. It came out of the frame; and I then saw—Bérangère had her back turned in my direction, so that not a detail escaped me—I then saw that there was inserted between the cardboard and the engraving a large sheet of paper covered with my uncle's writing.

At the top, in red ink, was a drawing of the three geometrical eyes.

Next came the following words, in bold black capitals:

"Instructions for working my discovery, abridged from the manuscript sent to my nephew."

65

And next forty or fifty very closely-written lines, in a hand too small to allow me to decipher them.

Besides, I had not the time. Bérangère merely glanced at the paper. Having found the object of her search and obtained possession of an additional document which my uncle had provided in case the manuscript should be lost, she folded it up, slipped it into her bodice, replaced the cardboard and hung the engraving where she had found it.

Was she going away? If so, she was bound to return as she had come, that is to say, evidently, through Noël Dorgeroux's dressing-room, on the other side of the bedroom, of which she had left the communicating-door ajar. I was about to prevent her and had already taken hold of the door-handle, when suddenly she moved a few steps towards my uncle's bed and fell on her knees, stretching out her hands in despair.

Her sobs rose in the silence. She stammered words which I was able to catch:

"God-father! ... My poor god-father!"

And she passionately kissed the coverlet of the bed beside which she must often have sat up watching my uncle when he was ill.

Her fit of crying lasted a long time and did not cease until just as I entered. Then she turned her head, saw me and stood up slowly, without taking her eyes from my face:

"You!" she murmured. "It's you!"

Seeing her make for the door, I said:

"Don't go, Bérangère."

She stopped, looking paler than ever, with drawn features.

"Give me that sheet of paper," I said, in a voice of command.

She handed it to me, with a quick movement. After a brief pause, I continued:

"Why did you come to fetch it? My uncle told you of its existence, didn't he? And you ... you were taking it to my uncle's murderers, so that they might have nothing more to fear and be the only persons to know the secret? ... Speak, Bérangère, will you?"

I had raised my voice and was advancing towards her. She took another step back.

"You shan't move, do you hear? Stay where you are. Listen to me and answer me!"

She made no further attempt to move. Her eyes were filled with such distress that I adopted a calmer demeanour:

"Answer me," I said, very gently. "You know that, whatever you may have done, I am your friend, your indulgent friend, and that I mean to help you ... and advise you. There are feelings which are proof against everything. Mine for you is of that sort. It is more than affection: you know it is, don't you, Bérangère? You know that I love you?"

Her lips quivered, she tried to speak, but could not. I repeated again and again:

"I love you! ... I love you!"

And, each time, she shuddered, as though these words, which I spoke with infinite emotion, which I had never spoken so seriously or so sincerely, as if these words wounded her in the very depths of her soul. What a strange creature she was!

I tried to put my hand on her shoulder. She avoided my friendly touch.

"What can you see to fear in me," I asked, "when I love you? Why not confess everything? You are not a free agent, are you? You are being forced to act as you do and you hate it all?"

Once more, anger was overmastering me. I was exasperated by her silence. I saw no way of compelling her to reply, of overcoming that incomprehensible obstinacy except by clasping her in my arms and yielding to the instinct of violence which urged me towards some brutal action.

I went boldly forward. But I had not taken a step before she spun round on her heel, so swiftly that I thought that she would drop to the floor in the doorway. I followed her into the other room. She uttered a terrible scream. At the same moment I was knocked down by a sudden blow. The man Massignac, who had been hiding in the dressing-room and watching us, had leapt at me and was attacking me furiously, while Bérangère fled to the staircase.

"Your daughter," I spluttered, defending myself, "your daughter! ... Stop her! ..."

The words were senseless, seeing that Massignac, beyond a doubt, was Bérangère's accomplice, or rather an inspiring force behind her, as indeed he proved by his determination to put me out of action, in order to protect his daughter against my pursuit.

We had rolled over the carpet and each of us was trying to master his adversary. The man Massignac was no longer laughing. He was striking harder blows than ever, but without using any weapon and without any murderous intent. I hit back as lustily and soon discovered that I was getting the better of him.

This gave me additional strength. I succeeded in flattening him beneath me. He stiffened every muscle to no purpose. We lay clutching each other, face to face, eye to eye. I took him by the throat and snarled:

"Ah, I shall get it out of you now, you wretch, and learn at last..."

And suddenly I ceased. My words broke off in a cry of horror and I clapped my hand to his face in such a way as to hide the lower part of it, leaving only the eyes visible. Oh, those eyes riveted on mine! Why, I knew them! Not with their customary expression of smug and hypocritical cheerfulness, but with the other expression which I was slowly beginning to remember. Yes, I remember them now, those two fierce, implacable eyes, filled with hatred and cruelty, those eyes which I had seen on the wall of the chapel, those eyes which had looked at me on that same day, when I lay gasping in the murderer's grip in the woods near the Yard.

And again, as on that occasion, suddenly my strength forsook me. Those savage eyes, those atrocious eyes, the man Massignac's real eyes, alarmed me.

He released himself with a laugh of triumph and, speaking in calm and deliberate accents, said:

"You're no match for me, young fellow! Don't you come meddling in my affairs again!"

Then, pushing me away, he ran off in the same direction as Bérangère.

A few minutes later, I perceived that the sheet of paper which the daughter had found behind the old engraving had been taken from me by the father; and then, but not till then, I understood the exact meaning of the attack.

The amphitheatre was duly inaugurated on the afternoon of that same day. Seated in the box-office was the manager of the establishment, the possessor of the great secret, Théodore Massignac, Noël Dorgeroux's murderer.

CHAPTER X

THE CROWD SEES

Théodore Massignac was installed at the box-office! Théodore Massignac, when a dispute of any kind occurred, left his desk and hastened to settle it! Théodore Massignac walked up and down, examining the tickets, showing people to their places, speaking a pleasant word here, giving a masterful order there and doing all these things with his everlasting smile and his obsequious graciousness.

Of embarrassment not the slightest sign. Everybody knew that Théodore Massignac was the fellow with the broad face and the wide-cleft mouth who was attracting the general attention. And everybody was fully aware that Théodore Massignac was the man of straw who had carried out the whole business and made away with Noël Dorgeroux. But nothing interfered with Théodore Massignac's jovial mood: not the sneers, nor the apparent hostility of the public, nor the more or less discreet supervision of the detectives attached to his person.

He had even had the effrontery to paste on boardings, to the right and left of the entrance, a pair of great posters representing Noël Dorgeroux's handsome face, with its grave and candid features!

These posters gave rise to a brief altercation between us. It was pretty lively, though it passed unnoticed by others. Scandalized by the sight of them, I went up to him, a little while before the time fixed for the opening; and, in a voice trembling with anger, said:

"Remove those at once. I will not have them displayed. The rest I don't care about. But this is too much of a good thing: it's a disgrace and an outrage."

He feigned an air of amazement:

"An outrage? You call it an outrage to honour your uncle's memory and to display the portrait of the talented inventor whose discovery is on the point of revolutionizing the world? I thought I was doing homage to him."

I was beside myself with rage:

"You shan't do it," I spluttered. "I will not consent, I will not consent to be an accomplice in your infamy."

"Oh, yes, you will!" he said, with a laugh. "You'll consent to this as you do to all the rest. It's all part of the game, young fellow. You've got to swallow it. You've got to swallow it because Uncle

Dorgeroux's fame must be made to soar above all these paltry trifles. Of course, I know, a word from you and I'm jugged. And then? What will become of the great invention? In the soup, that's where it'll be, my lad, because I am the sole possessor of all the secrets and all the formulae. The sole possessor, do you understand? Friend Velmot, the man with the glasses, is only a super, a tool. So is Bérangère. Therefore, with Théodore Massignac put away, there's an end of the astounding pictures signed 'Dorgeroux.' No more glory, no more immortality. Is that what you want, young man?"

Without waiting for any reply, he added:

"And then there's something else; a word or two which I overheard last night. Ha, ha, my dear sir, so we're in love with Bérangère! We're prepared to defend her against all dangers! Well, in that case—do be logical—what have I to fear? If you betray me, you betray your sweetheart. Come, am I right or wrong? Daddy and his little girl ... hand and glove, you might say. If you cut off one, what becomes of the other? ... Ah, you're beginning to understand! You'll be good now, won't you? There, that's much better! We shall see a happy ending yet, you'll have heaps of children crowding round your knee and who will thank me then for getting him a nice little settlement? Why, Victorien!"

He stopped and watched me, with a jeering air. Clenching my fists, I shouted, furiously:

"You villain!... Oh, what a villain you make yourself appear!"

But some people were coming up and he turned his back on me, after whispering:

"Hush, Victorien! Don't insult your father-in-law elect."

I restrained myself. The horrible brute was right. I was condemned to silence by motives so powerful that Théodore Massignac would soon be able to fulfil his task without having to fear the least revolt of conscience on my part. Noël Dorgeroux and Bérangère were watching over him.

Meanwhile, the amphitheatre was filling; and the motorcars continued to arrive in swift succession, pouring forth the torrent of privileged people who, because of their wealth or their position, had paid from ten to twenty louis for a seat. Financiers, millionaires, famous actresses, newspaper-proprietors, artistic and literary celebrities, Anglo-Saxon commercial magnates, secretaries of great labour unions, all flocked with a sort of fever towards that unknown spectacle, of which no detailed programme was obtainable and which they were not even certain of beholding, since it was impossible to say whether Noël Dorgeroux's processes had really been recovered and employed in the right way. Indeed, no one, among those who believed the story, was in a position to declare that Théodore Massignac had not taken advantage of the whole business in order to arrange the most elaborate hoax. The very tickets and posters contained the anything but reassuring words:

> "In the event of unfavourable weather, the tickets will be available for the following day. Should the exhibition be prevented by any other cause, the money paid for the seats will not be refunded; and no claims to that effect can be entertained."

Yet nothing had restrained the tremendous outburst of curiosity. Whether confident or suspicious, people insisted on being there. Besides, the weather was fine. The sun shone out of a cloudless sky. Why not indulge in the somewhat anxious gaiety that filled the hearts of the crowd?

Everything was ready. Thanks to his wonderful activity and his remarkable powers of organization, Théodore Massignac, assisted by architects and contractors and acting on the plans worked out, had completed and revised Noël Dorgeroux's work. He had recruited a numerous staff, especially a large and stalwart body of men, who, as I heard, were lavishly paid and who were charged with the duty of keeping order.

As for the amphitheatre, built of reinforced concrete, it was completely filled up, well laid out and very comfortable. Twelve rows of elbowed seats, supplied with movable cushions, surrounded a floor which rose in a gentle slope, divided into twelve tiers arranged in a wide semicircle. Behind these was a series of spacious private boxes, and, at the back of all, a lounge, the floor of which, nevertheless, was not more than ten or twelve feet above the level of the ground.

Opposite was the wall.

It stood well away from the seats, being built on a foundation of masonry and separated from the spectators by an empty orchestra. Furthermore, a grating, six feet high, prevented access to the wall, at least as regards its central portion; and, when I say a grating, I mean a businesslike grating, with spiked rails and cross-bars forming too close a mesh to allow of the passage of a man's arm.

The central part was the screen, which was raised to about the level of the fourth or fifth tier of seats. Two pilasters, standing at eight or ten yards' distance from each other, marked its boundaries and supported an overhanging canopy. For the moment, all this space was masked by an iron curtain, roughly daubed with gaudy landscapes and ill-drawn views.

At half-past three there was not a vacant seat nor an unoccupied corner. The police had ordered the doors to be closed. The crowd was beginning to grow impatient and to give signs of a certain irritability, which betrayed itself in the hum of a thousand voices, in nervous laughter and in jests which were becoming more and more caustic.

"If the thing goes wrong," said a man by my side, "we shall see a shindy."

I had taken up my stand, with some journalists of my acquaintance, in the lounge, amid a noisy multitude which was all the more peevish inasmuch as it was not comfortably seated like the audience in the stalls.

Another journalist, who was invariably well-informed and of whom I had seen a good deal lately, replied:

"Yes, there will be a shindy; but that is not the worthy Massignac's principal danger. He is risking something besides."

"What?" I asked.

"Arrest."

"Do you mean that?"

"I do. If the universal curiosity, which has helped him to preserve his liberty so far, is satisfied, he's all right. If not, if he fails, he'll be locked up. The warrant is out."

I shuddered. Massignac's arrest implied the gravest possible peril to Bérangère.

"And you may be sure," my acquaintance continued, "that he is fully alive to what is hanging over his head and that he is feeling anything but chirpy at heart."

"At heart, perhaps," replied one of the others. "But he doesn't allow it to appear on the surface. There, look at him: did you ever see such swank?"

A louder din had come from the crowd. Below us, Théodore Massignac was walking along the pit and crossing the empty space of the orchestra. He was accompanied by a dozen of those sturdy fellows who composed the male staff of the amphitheatre. He made them sit down on two benches which were evidently reserved for them and, with the most natural air, gave them his instructions. And his gestures so clearly denoted the sense of the orders imparted and expressed so clearly what they would have to do if any one attempted to approach the wall that a loud clamour of protest arose.

Massignac turned towards the audience, without appearing in the least put out, and, with a smiling face, gave a careless shrug of the shoulders, as though to say:

"What's the trouble? I'm taking precautions. Surely I'm entitled to do that!"

And, retaining his bantering geniality, he took a key from his waist-coat pocket, opened a little gate in the railing and entered the last enclosure before the wall.

This manner of playing the lion-tamer who takes refuge behind the bars of his cage made so comic an impression that the hisses became mingled with bursts of laughter.

"The worthy Massignac is right," said my friend the journalist, in a tone of approval. "In this way he avoids either of two things: if he fails, the malcontents won't be able to break his head; and, if he succeeds, the enthusiasts can't make a rush for the wall and learn the secret of the hoax. He's a knowing one. He has prepared for everything."

There was a stool in the fortified enclosure. Théodore Massignac sat down on it half facing the spectators, some four paces in front of the wall, and, holding his watch towards us, tapped it with his other hand to explain that the decisive hour was about to strike.

The extension of time which he thus obtained lasted for some minutes. But then the uproar began anew and became deafening. People suddenly lost all confidence. The idea of a hoax took possession of every mind, all the more as people were unable to grasp why the spectacle should begin at any particular time rather than another, since it all depended solely on Théodore Massignac.

"Curtain! Curtain!" they cried.

After a moment, not so much in obedience to this order as because the hands of his watch seemed to command it, he rose, went to the wall, slipped back a wooden slab which covered two electric pushes and pressed one of them with his finger.

The iron curtain descended slowly and sank into the ground.

The screen appeared in its entirety, in broad daylight and of larger proportions than the ordinary.

I shuddered before this flat surface, over which the mysterious coating was spread in a dark-grey layer. And the same tremor ran through the crowd, which was also seized with the recollection of my depositions. Was it possible that we were about to behold one of those extraordinary spectacles the story of which had given rise to so much controversial discussion? How ardently I longed for it! At this solemn minute, I forget all the phases of the drama, all the loathing that I felt for Massignac, all that had to do with Bérangère, the madness of her actions, the anguish of my love, and thought only of the great game that was being played around my uncle's discovery. Would what I had seen vanish in the darkness of the past which I myself, the sole witness of the miracles, was beginning to doubt? Or would the incredible vision arise once again and yet

73

again, to teach the future the name of Noël Dorgeroux? Had I been right in sacrificing to the victim's glory the vengeance called for by his death? Or had I made myself the accomplice of the murderer in not denouncing his abominable crime?

Yes, I was becoming his accomplice and even, deep down in my consciousness, his collaborator and his ally. Had I imagined that Massignac had need of me, I would have hastened to his side. I would have encouraged him with all my confidence and assisted him to the full extent of my ability. First and foremost I wished him to emerge victoriously from the struggle which he had undertaken. I wanted my uncle's secret to come to life again. I wanted light to spring from the shadow. I did not wish twenty years of study and the supreme idea of that most noble genius to be flung back into the abyss.

Now not a sound broke the profound silence. The people's faces were set. Their eyes pierced the wall like so many gimlets. They experienced in their turn the anxiety of my own waiting for that which was yet invisible and which was preparing in the depths of the mysterious substance. And the implacable will of a thousand spectators united with that of Massignac, who stood there below, with his back bent and his head thrust forward; wildly questioning the impassive horizon of the wall.

He was the first to see the first premonitory gleam. A cry escaped his lips, while his two hands frantically beat the air. And, almost at the same second, like sparks crackling on every side, other cries were scattered in the silence, which was instantly restored, heavier and denser than before.

The Three Eyes were there.

The Three Eyes marked their three curved triangles on the wall.

The onlookers had not, in the presence of this inconceivable phenomenon, to submit to the sort of initiation through which I had passed. To them, from the outset, three geometrical figures, dismal and lifeless though they were, represented three eyes; to them also they were living eyes even before they became animated. And the excitement was intense when those lidless eyes, consisting of hard, symmetrical lines, suddenly became filled with an expression which made them as intelligible to us as the eyes of a human person.

It was a harsh, proud expression, containing flashes of malignant joy. And I knew—and we all knew—that this was not just a random expression, with which the Three Eyes had been arbitrarily endowed, but that of a being who looked upon real life with that same look and who was about to appear to us in real life.

Then, as always, the three figures began to revolve dizzily. The disk turned upon itself. And everything was interrupted. . . .

74

CHAPTER XI

THE CATHEDRAL

The crowd could not recover from its stupefaction. It sat and waited. It had heard through me of the Three Eyes, of their significance as a message, a preliminary illustration, something like the title or picture-poster of the coming spectacle. It remembered Edith Cavell's eyes, Philippe Dorgeroux's eyes, Bérangère's eyes, all those eyes which I had seen again afterwards; and it sat as though cramped in obstinate silence, as though it feared lest a word or a movement should scare away the invisible god who lay hidden within the wall. It was now filled with absolute certainty. This first proof of my sincerity and perspicacity was enough; there was not a single unbeliever left. The spectators stepped straight into regions which I had reached only by painful stages. Not a shadow of protest impaired their sensibility. Not a doubt interfered with their faith. Really, I saw around me nothing but serious attention, restrained enthusiasm, suppressed exaltation.

And all this suddenly found vent in an immense shout that rose to the skies. Before us, on the screen which had but now been empty and bare as a stretch of sand, there had come into being, spontaneously, in a flash, hundreds and thousands of men, swarming in unspeakable confusion.

It was obviously the suddenness and complexity of the sight which so profoundly stirred the crowd. The sudden emergence of life innumerable out of nothingness convulsed it like an electric shock. In front of it, where there had been nothing, there now swarmed another crowd, dense as itself, a crowd whose excitement mingled with its own and whose uproar, which it was able to divine, was added to its own! For a few seconds I had the impression that it was losing its mental balance and swaying to and fro in an access of delirium.

However, the crowd once more regained its self-control. The need, not of understanding—it seemed not to care about that at first—but of seeing and grasping the entire manifestation of the phenomena mastered the force let loose in its midst. It became silent again. It gazed. And it listened.

Yonder—I dare not say on the screen, for, in truth, so abnormal were its dimensions that the picture overflowed the frame and was propelled into the space outside—yonder, that which had impressed us as being disorder and chaos became organized in accordance with a certain rhythm which at length grew perceptible to us. The movement to and fro was that of artisans performing a well-regulated task; and the task was accomplished about an immense fabric in the course of erection.

How all these artisans were clad in a fashion absolutely different from our own; and, on the other hand, the tools which they employed, the appearance of their ladders, the shape of their scaffoldings, their manner of carrying loads and of hoisting the necessary materials in wicker baskets to the upper floors, all these things, together with a multitude of further details, brought us into the heart of a period which must have been the thirteenth or fourteenth century.

There were numbers of monks supervising the works, calling out orders from one end of the vast site to the other, setting out measurements and not disdaining themselves to mix the mortar, to push a wheel-barrow or to saw a stone. Women of the people, uttering their cries at the top of their voices, walked about bearing jars of wine with which they filled cups that were at once emptied by the thirsty labourers. A beggar went by. Two tattered singers began to roar a ditty, accompanying themselves on a sort of guitar. And a troop of acrobats, all lacking an arm, or a leg, or both legs, were preparing to give their show, when the scene changed without any transition, like a stage setting which is altered by the mere pressure of a button.

What we now saw was the same picture of a building in process of construction. But this time we clearly distinguished the plan of the edifice, the whole base of a Gothic cathedral displaying its huge proportions. And on these courses of masonry, which had reached the lower level of the towers, and along the fronts and before the niches and on the steps of the porch, everywhere, in fact, swarmed stone-hewers, masons, sculptors, carpenters, apprentices and monks.

And the costumes were no longer the same. A century or two had passed.

Next came a series of pictures which succeeded one another without our being able to separate the one from the other or to ascribe a beginning or an end to any one of them. By a method no doubt similar to that which, on the cinematograph, shows us the growth of a plant, we saw the cathedral rising imperceptibly, blossoming like a flower whose exquisitely-moulded petals open one by one and, lastly, being completed before our eyes, all of itself, without any human intervention. Thus came a moment when it stood out against the sky in all its glory and harmonious strength. It was Rheims Cathedral, with its three recessed doorways, its host of statues, its magnificent rose-windows, its wonderful towers flanked by airy turrets, its flying buttresses and the lacework of its carvings and balconies, Rheims Cathedral such as the centuries had beheld it, before its mutilation by the Huns.

A long shudder passed through the crowd. It understood what those who were not present cannot easily be made to understand now, by means of insignificant words: it understood that in front of it there stood something other than the photographic presentment of a building; and, as it possessed the profound and accurate intuition that it was not the victim of an unthinkable hoax, it became imbued and overwhelmed by an utterly disturbing sense of witnessing a most prodigious spectacle: the actual erection of a church in the Middle Ages, the actual work of a thirteenth-century building-yard, the actual life of the monks and artists who built Rheims Cathedral. Enlightened by its subtle instinct, not for a second did it doubt the evidence of its eyes. What I had denied, or at least what I had admitted only as an illusion, with reservations and flashes of incredulity, the crowd accepted with a certainty against which it would have been madness to rebel. It had faith. It believed with religious fervour. What it saw was not an artificial evocation of the past but that past itself, revived in all its living reality.

Equally real was the gradual transformation which continued to take place, no longer in the actual lines of the building, but as one might say in its substance and which was revealed by progressive changes that could not be attributed to any other cause than that of time. The great white mass grew darker. The grain of the stones became worn and weathered and they assumed that appearance of rugged bark which the patient gnawing of the years is apt to give them. It is true, the cathedral did not grow old, yet lived, for age is the beauty and the youth of the stones by means of which man gives shape to his dreams.

It lived and breathed through the centuries, seeming all the fresher as it faded and the more ornate as its legions of saints and angels became mutilated. It chanted its solemn hymn into the open sky over the houses which had gradually concealed its doorways and aisles, over the town above whose crowded roofs it towered, over the plains and hills which formed the dim horizon.

At different times people came and leant against the balustrade of some lofty balcony or appeared in the frame of the tall windows; and the costume of these people enabled us to note their successive periods. Thus we saw pre-Revolutionary citizens, followed by soldiers of the Empire, who in turn were followed by other nineteenth-century civilians and by labourers building scaffoldings and by yet more labourers engaged in the work of restoration.

Then a final vision appeared before our eyes: a group of French officers in service uniform. They hurriedly reached the top of the tower, looked through their field-glasses and went down again. Here and there, over the town and the country, hovered those small, woolly clouds which mark the bursting of a shell.

The silence of the crowd became anguished. Their eyes stared apprehensively. We all felt what was coming and we were all judging as a whole a spectacle which had shown us the gradual birth and marvellous growth of the cathedral only by way of leading up to the dramatic climax. We expected this climax. It followed from the dominant idea which gave the film its unity and its raison d'être. It was as logical as the last act of a Greek tragedy. But how could we forsee all the savage grandeur and all the horror contained in that climax? How could we forsee that the bombardment of Rheims Cathedral itself formed part of the climax only as a preparation and that, beyond the violent and sensational scene which was about to rack our nerves and shock our minds, there would follow yet another scene of the most terrible nature, a scene which was strictly accurate in every detail?

The first shell fell on the north-east part of the cathedral at a spot which we could not see, because the building, though we were looking down upon it from a slight elevation, presented only its west front to our eyes. But a flame shot up, like a flash of lightning, and a pillar of smoke whirled into the cloudless sky.

And, almost simultaneously, three more shells followed, three more explosives, mingling their puffs of smoke. A fifth fell a little more forward, in the middle of the roof. A mighty flame arose. Rheims Cathedral was on fire.

Then followed phenomena which are really inexplicable in the present state of our cinematographic resources. I say cinematographic, although the term is not perhaps strictly accurate; but I do not know how else to describe the miraculous visions of the Yard. Nor do I know of any comparison to employ when speaking of the visible parabola of the sixth shell, which we followed with our eyes through space and which even stopped for a moment, to resume its leisurely course and to stop again at a few inches from the statue which it was about to strike. This was a charming and ingenuous statue of a saint lifting her arms to God, with the sweetest, happiest and most trusting expression on her face; a masterpiece of grace and beauty; a divine creature who had stood for centuries, cloistered in her shelter, among the nests of the swallows, living her humble life of prayer and adoration, and who now smiled at the death that threatened her. A flash, a puff of smoke... and, in the place of the little saint and her daintily-carved niche, a yawning gap!

It was at this moment that I felt that anger and hatred were awakening all around me. The murder of the little saint had roused the indignation of the crowd; and it so happened that this indignation found an occasion to express itself. Before us, the cathedral grew smaller, while at the same time it approached us. It seemed to be leaving its frame, while the distant landscape came nearer and nearer. A hill, bristling with barbed wire, dug with trenches and strewn with corpses, rose and fell away; and we saw its top, which was fortified with bastions and cupolas of reinforced concrete.

Enormous guns displayed their long barrels. A multitude of German soldiers were moving swiftly to and fro. It was the battery which was shelling Rheims Cathedral.

In the centre stood a group of general officers, field-glasses in hand, with sword-belts unbuckled. At each shot, they watched the effect through their glasses and then nodded their heads with an air of satisfaction.

But a great commotion now took place among them. They drew up in single rank, assuming a stiff and automatic attitude, while the soldiers continued to serve the guns. And suddenly, from behind the fortress, a motor-car appeared, accompanied by an escort of cavalry. It stopped on the emplacement and from it there alighted a man wearing a helmet and a long fur-cloak, which was lifted at the side by the scabbard of a sword of which he held the hilt. He stepped briskly to the foreground. We recognised the Kaiser.

He shook hands with one of the generals. The others saluted more stiffly than ever and then, at a sign from their master, extended and formed a semicircle around him and the general whose hand he had shaken.

A conversation ensued. The general, after an explanation accompanied by gestures that pointed towards the town, called for a telescope and had it correctly pointed. The Kaiser put his eye to it.

One of the guns was ready. The order to fire was given.

Two pictures followed each other on the screen in quick succession: that of a carved stone balustrade smashed to pieces by the shell and that of the emperor drawing himself up immediately afterwards. He had seen! He had seen; and his face, which appeared to us suddenly enlarged and alone upon the screen, beamed with intense delight!

He began to talk volubly. His sensual lips, his upturned moustache, his wrinkled and fleshy cheeks were all moving at the same time. But, when another gun was obviously on the point of firing, he held his peace and looked in the direction of the town. Just then he raised his hand to a level just below his eyes, so that we saw them by themselves, between the hand and the peak of the helmet. They were hard, evil, proud, implacable. They wore the expression of the miraculous Three Eyes that had throbbed before us on the screen.

They lit up, glittering with an evil smile. They saw what we saw at the same time, a whole block of capitals and cornices falling to the ground and more flames rising in angry pillars of fire. Then the emperor burst out laughing. One picture showed him doubled up in two and holding his sides amid the group of generals all seized with the same uncontrollable laughter. He was laughing! He was laughing! It was so amusing! Rheims Cathedral was ablaze! The venerable fabric to which the kings of France used to come for their coronation was falling into ruins! The might of Germany was striking the enemy in his very heart! The German heavy guns were things that were noble and beautiful! And it was he who had ordained it, he, the emperor, the King of Prussia, master of the world, William of Hohenzollern! .... Oh, the joy of laughing his fill, laughing to his heart's content, laughing the frank, honest laughter of a jolly German!

A storm of hoots and hisses broke loose in the amphitheatre. The crowd had risen in a body, shaking their fists and bellowing forth insults. The attendants had to struggle with a troop of angry men who had invaded the orchestra.

Théodore Massignac, behind the bars of his cage, stooped and pressed the button.

The iron curtain rose.

CHAPTER XII

THE "SHAPES"

On the morning of the day following this memorable spectacle, I woke late, after a feverish night during which I twice seemed to hear the sound of a shot.

"Nightmare!" I thought, when I got up. "I was haunted by the pictures of the bombardment; and what I heard was the bursting of the shells."

The explanation was plausible enough: the powerful emotions of the amphitheatre, coming after my meeting with Bérangère in the course of that other night and my struggle with Théodore Massignac, had thrown me into a state of nervous excitement. But, when I entered the room in which my coffee was served, Théodore Massignac came running in, carrying a heap of newspapers which he threw on the table; and I saw under his hat a bandage which hid his forehead. Had he been wounded? And was I to believe that there had really been shots fired in the Yard?

"Pay no attention," he said; "a mere scratch. I've bruised myself." And, pointing to the newspapers: "Read that, rather. It's all about the master's triumph."

I made no protest against the loathsome brute's intrusion. The Master's triumph, as he said, and Bérangère's safety compelled me to observe a silence by which he was to benefit until the completion of his plans. He had made himself at home in Noël Dorgeroux's house; and his attitude showed that he was alive to his own rights and to my helplessness. Nevertheless, despite his arrogance, he seemed to me to be anxious and absorbed. He no longer laughed; and, without his cheery laugh, Théodore Massignac disconcerted me more than ever.

"Yes," he continued, drawing himself up, "it's a victory, a victory accepted by everybody. Not one of all these articles strikes a false note. Bewilderment and enthusiasm, stupefaction and high-flown praises, all running riot together. They're everyone of them alike; and, on the other hand, there is no attempt at a plausible explanation. Those fellows are all astounded. They're like blind men walking without a stick. Well, well, it's a thick-headed world!"

He came and stood in front of me and, bluntly:

"What then?" he said. "Can't you guess? It's really too funny! Now that I understand the affair, I'm petrified by the idea that people don't see through it. An unprecedented discovery, I agree, and yet so simple! And, even then, you can hardly call it a discovery. For, when all is said and done ... Look here, the whole story is so completely within the capacity of the first-comer that it won't take long to clear it up. To-morrow or the next day, some one will say, 'The trick of the Yard?' I've got it! And that's that. You don't want to be a man of learning for that, believe me. On the contrary!"

He shrugged his shoulders:

"And besides, I don't care. Let them find out what they like: they'll still need the formula; and that's hidden in my cellar and nowhere else. Nobody knows it, not even our friend Velmot. Noël Dorgeroux's steel plate? Melted down. The instructions which he left at the back of D'Alembert's portrait? Burnt to ashes. So there's no danger of any competition. And, as the seats in the amphitheatre are selling like hot cakes, I shall have pocketed a million in less than a fortnight, two millions in less than three weeks. And then good-bye, gentlemen all, I'm off. By Jove! It won't do to tempt Providence or the gendarmes."

He took me by the lapels of my jacket and, standing straight in front of me, with his eyes on mine, said, in a more serious voice:

"There's only one thing that would ruffle me, which is to think that all these beautiful pictures can no longer appear upon the screen when I am gone. It seems impossible, what? No more miraculous sights? No more fairy-tales to make people talk till Doomsday? That would never do, would it? Noël Dorgeroux's secret must not be lost. So I thought of you. Hang it, you're his nephew! Besides, you love my dear Bérangère. Some day or other you'll be married to her. And then, as I'm working for her, it doesn't matter whether the money comes to her through you or through me, does it? Listen to me, Victorien Beaugrand, and remember every word I say. Listen to me. You've observed that the base of the wall below the screen stands out a good way. Noël Dorgeroux contrived a sort of recess there, containing several carboys, filled with different substances, and a copper vat. In this vat we mix certain quantities of those ingredients in fixed proportions, adding a fluid from a little phial prepared on the morning of the performances, according to your uncle's formula. Then, an hour or two before sunset, we dip a big brush in the wash thus obtained and daub the surface of the screen very evenly with it. You do that for each performance, if you want the pictures to be clear, and of course only on days when there are no clouds between the sun and the screen. As for the formula, it is not very long: fifteen letters and twelve figures in all, like this ..."

Massignac repeated slowly, in a less decided tone:

"Fifteen letters and twelve figures. Once you know them by heart, you can be easy. And I too. Yes, what do I risk in speaking to you? You swear that you won't tell, eh? And then I hold you through Bérangère. Well, those fifteen letters...."

He was obviously hesitating. His words seemed to cost him an increasing effort; and suddenly he pushed me back, struck the table angrily with his fist and cried:

"Well, no, then, no, no, no! I shall not speak. It would be too silly! No, I shall keep this thing in my own hands, yes! Is it likely that I should let the business go for two millions? Not for ten millions! Not for twenty! I shall mount guard for months, if necessary, as I did last night, with my gun on my shoulder ... and if any one enters the Yard I'll shoot him as I would a dog. The wall belongs to me, Théodore Massignac. Hands off! Let no one dare to touch it! Let no one try to rob me of the least scrap of it! It's my secret! It's my formula! I bought the goods and risked my neck in doing it. I'll defend them to my last breath; and, if I kick the bucket, it can't be helped; I'll carry them with me to the grave!"

He shook his fist at invisible enemies. Then suddenly, he caught hold of me again: "That's what things have come to. My arrest, the gendarmes ... I don't care a hang. They'll never dare. But the thief lurking in the darkness, the murderer who fires at me, as he did last night, while I was mounting guard.... For you must have heard, Victorien Beaugrand? Oh, a mere scratch! And I missed him too. But, next time, the swine will give himself time to take aim at me. Oh, the filthy swine!"

He began to shake me violently to and fro.

"But you too, Victorien, he's your enemy too! Don't you understand? The man with the eye-glass? That scoundrel Velmot? He wants to steal my secret, but he also wants to rob you of the girl you love. Sooner or later, you'll have your hands full with him, just as I have. Won't you defend yourself, you damned milksop, and attack him when you get the chance? Suppose I told you that Bérangère's in love with him? Aha, that makes you jump! You're not blind surely? Can't you see for yourself that it was for him she was working all the winter and that, if I hadn't put a stop to it, I should have been diddled? She's in love with him, Victorien. She is the handsome Velmot's obedient slave. Why don't you smash his swanking mug for him? He's here. He's prowling about in the village. I saw him last night. Blast it, if I could only put a bullet through the beast's skin!"

Massignac spat out a few more oaths, mingled with offensive epithets which were aimed at myself as much as at Velmot. He described his daughter as a jade and a dangerous madwoman, threatened to kill me if I committed the least indiscretion and at length, with his mouth full of insults and his fists clenched, walked out backwards, like a man who fears a final desperate assault from his adversary.

He had nothing to be afraid of. I remained impassive under the storm of abuse. The only things that had roused me were his accusation against Bérangère and his blunt declaration of her love for the man Velmot. But I had long since resolved not to take my feelings for her into account, to ignore them entirely, not even to defend her or condemn her or judge her and to refuse to accept my suffering until events had afforded me undeniable proofs. I knew her to be guilty of acts which I did not know of. Was I therefore to believe her guilty of those of which she was accused?

At heart, the feeling that seemed to persist was a profound pity. The horrible tragedy in which Bérangère was submerged was increasing in violence. Théodore Massignac and his accomplice were now antagonists. Once again Noël Dorgeroux's secret was about to cause an outburst of passion; and everything seemed to foretell that Bérangère would be swept away in the storm.

What I read in the newspapers confirmed what Massignac had told me. The articles lie before me as I write. They all express the same, more or less pugnacious, enthusiasm; and none of them gives a forecast of the truth which nevertheless was on the point of being discovered. While the ignorant and superficial journalists go wildly to work, heaping up the most preposterous suppositions, the really cultivated writers maintain a great reserve and appear to be mainly concerned in resisting any idea of a miracle to which a section of the public might be inclined to give ear:

"There is no miracle about it!" they exclaim. "We are in the presence of a scientific riddle which will be solved by purely scientific means. In the meantime let us confess our total incompetence."

In any case, the comments of the press could not fail to increase the public excitement to the highest degree. At six o'clock in the evening the amphitheatre was taken by assault. The wholly inadequate staff vainly attempted to stop the invasion of the crowd. Numbers of seats were occupied by main force by people who had no right to be there; and the performance began in tumult and confusion, amid the hostile clamour and mad applause that greeted the man Massignac when he passed through the bars of his cage.

True, the crowd lapsed into silence as soon as the Three Eyes appeared, but it remained nervous and irritable; and the spectacle that followed was not one to alleviate those symptoms. It was a strange spectacle, the most difficult to understand of all those which

I saw. In the case of the others, those which preceded and those which followed, the mystery lay solely in the fact of their presentment. We beheld normal, natural scenes. But this one showed us things that are contrary to the things that are, things that might happen in the nightmare of a madman or in the hallucinations of a man dying in delirium.

I hardly know how to speak of it without myself appearing to have lost my reason; and I really should not dare to do so if a thousand others had not witnessed the same grotesque phantasmagoria and above all if this crazy vision—it is the only possible adjective—had not happened to be precisely the determining cause which set the public in the track of truth.

A thousand witnesses, I said, but I admit, a thousand witnesses who subsequently differed in their evidence, thanks to the inconsistency of the impressions received and also to the rapidity with which they succeeded one another.

And I myself, what did I see, after all? Animated shapes. Yes, that and nothing more. Living shapes. Every visible thing has a shape. A rock, a pyramid, a scaffolding round a house has a shape; but you cannot say that they are alive. Now this thing was alive. This thing bore perhaps no closer relation to the shape of a live being than to the shape of a rock, a pyramid or a scaffolding. Nevertheless there was no doubt that this thing acted in the manner of a being which lives, moves, follows this or that direction, obeys individual motives and attains a chosen goal.

I will not attempt to describe these shapes. How indeed could I do so, considering that they all differed from one another and that they even differed from themselves within the space of a second! Imagine a sack of coal (the comparison is forced upon one by the black and lumpy appearance of the Shapes), imagine a sack of coal swelling into the body of an ox, only to shrink at once to the proportions of the body of a dog, and next to grow thicker or to draw itself out lengthwise. Imagine this mass, which has no more consistency than a jellyfish, now again putting forth three little tentacles, resembling hands. Lastly, imagine the picture of a town, a town which is not horizontal but perpendicular, with streets standing up like ladders and, along these arteries, the Shapes rising like balloons. This is the first vision; and, right at the top of the town, the Shapes come crowding from every side, gathering upon a vast horizontal space, where they swarm like ants.

I receive the impression—and it is the general impression—that the space is a public square. A mound marks its centre. Shapes are standing there motionless. Others approach by means of successive dilations and contractions, which appear to constitute their method of advancing. And in this way, on the passage of a group of no great dimensions, which seems to be carrying a lifeless Shape, the multitude of the living Shapes falls back.

What happens next? However clear my sensations may be, however precise the memory which I have retained of them, I hesitate to write them down in so many words. I repeat, the vision transcends the limits of absurdity, while provoking a shudder of horror of which you are conscious without understanding it. For, after all what does it mean? Two powerful Shapes protrude their three tentacles, which wind themselves round the lifeless Shape that has been brought up, crush it, rend it, compress it and, rising in the air, wave to and fro a small mass which they have separated, like a severed head, from the original Shape and which contains the geometrical Three Eyes, staring, void of eyelids, void of expression.

No, it means nothing. It is a series of unconnected, unreal visions. And yet our hearts are wrung with anguish, as though we had been present at a murder or an execution. And yet those incoherent visions were perhaps what contributed most to the discovery of the truth. Their absence of logic brought about a logical explanation of the phenomena. The excessive darkness kindled a first glimmer of light.

To-day those things which, in looking up the past, I describe as incoherent and dark seem to me quite orderly and absolutely clear. But on that late afternoon, with a storm brewing in the distant sky, the crowd, recovering from its painful emotion, became more noisy and more aggressive. The exhibition had disappointed the spectators. They had not found what they expected and they manifested their dissatisfaction by threatening cries aimed at Théodore Massignac. The incidents that were to mark the sudden close of the performance were preparing.

"Mas-si-gnac! Mas-si-gnac!" they shouted, in chorus.

Standing in the middle of his cage, with his head turned towards the screen, he was watching for possible premonitory signs of a fresh picture. And, as a matter of fact, if you looked carefully, the signs were there. One might say that, rather than pictures, there were reflections of pictures skimming over the surface of the wall like faint clouds.

Suddenly Massignac extended one arm. The faint clouds were assuming definite outlines; and we saw that, under this mist, the spectacle had begun anew and was continuing.

But it continued as though under difficulties, with intervals of total suspension and others of semi-darkness during which the visions were covered by a mist. At such moments we saw almost deserted streets in which most of the shops were closed. There was no one at the doors or windows.

A cart, of which we caught sight now and again, moved along these streets. It contained, in front, two gendarmes dressed as in the days of the Revolution and, at the back, a priest and a man in a full-skirted coat, dark breeches and white stockings.

An isolated picture showed us the man's head and shoulders. I recognised and, generally speaking, the whole audience in the amphitheatre recognised the heavy-jowled face of King Louis XVI. This expression was hard and proud.

We saw him again, after a few interruptions, in a great square surrounded by artillery and black with soldiers. He climbed the steep steps of a scaffold. His coat and neck-tie had been removed. The priest was supporting him. Four executioners tried to lay hold of him.

I am obliged to interrupt my narrative, which I am deliberately wording as drily as possible, of these fleeting apparitions, in order to make it quite clear that they did not at the moment produce the effect of terror which my readers might suppose. They were too short, too desultory, let me say, and so bad from the strictly cinematographic point of view which the audience adopted, in spite of itself, that they excited irritation and annoyance rather than dread.

The spectators had suddenly lost all confidence. They laughed, they sang. They hooted Massignac. And the storm of invective increased when, on the screen, one of the executioners held up the head of the king and faded away in the mist, together with the scaffold, the soldiers and the guns.

There were a few more timid attempts at pictures, attempts on the part of the film, in which several persons say that they recognized Queen Marie Antoinette, attempts which sustained the patience of the onlookers who were anxious to see the end of a spectacle which they had paid so heavily to attend. But the violence could no longer be restrained.

Who started it? Who was the first to rush forward and provoke the disorder and the resultant panic? The subsequent enquiries failed to show. There seems no doubt that the whole crowd obeyed its impulse to give full expression to its dissatisfaction and that the more turbulent of its members seized the opportunity of belabouring Théodore Massignac and even of trying to take the fabulous screen by storm. This last attempt, at any rate, failed before the impenetrable rampart formed by the attendants, who, armed with knuckledusters or truncheons, repelled the flood of the invaders. As for Massignac, who, after raising the curtain, had the unfortunate idea of leaving his cage and running to one of the exits, he was struck as he passed and swallowed up in the angry swirl of rioters.

After that everybody attacked his neighbour, with a frantic desire for strife and violence which brought into conflict not only the enemies of Massignac and the partisans of order, but also those who were exasperated and those who had no thought but of escaping from the turmoil. Sticks and umbrellas were brandished on high. Women seized one another by the hair. Blood flowed. People fell to the ground, wounded.

I myself did my best to get out and shouldered my way through this indescribable fray. It was no easy work, for numbers of policemen and many people who had not been able to obtain entrance were thronging towards the exit-doors of the amphitheatre. At last I succeeded in reaching the gate through an opening that was made amid the crowd.

"Room for the wounded man!" a tall, clean-shaven fellow was shouting, in a stentorian voice.

Two others followed, carrying in their arms an individual covered with rugs and overcoats.

The crowd fell back. The little procession moved out. I seized my opportunity.

The tall fellow pointed to a private motor-car waiting outside:

"Chauffeur, I'm requisitioning you. Orders of the prefect of police. Come along, the two of you, and get a move on!"

The two men put the victim into the car and took their places inside. The tall fellow sat down beside the chauffeur; and the car drove off.

It was not until the very second when it turned the corner that I conceived in a flash and without any reason whatever the exact idea of what this little scene meant. Suddenly I guessed the identity of the wounded man who was hidden so attentively and carried off so assiduously. And suddenly also, notwithstanding the change of face, though he wore neither beard nor glasses, I gave a name to the tall, clean-shaven fellow. It was the man Velmot.

I rushed back to the Yard and informed the commissary of police who had hitherto had charge of the Dorgeroux case. He whistled up his men. They leapt into taxi-cabs and cars. It was too late. The roads were already filled with such a block of traffic that the commissary's car was unable to move.

And thus, in the very midst of the crowd, by means of the most daring stratagem, taking advantage of a crush which he himself doubtless had his share in bringing about, the man Velmot had carried off his confederate and implacable enemy, Théodore Massignac.

CHAPTER XIII

THE VEIL IS LIFTED

I will not linger over the two films of this second performance and the evident connection between them. At the present moment we are too near the close of this extraordinary story to waste time over minute, tedious, unimportant details. We must remember that, on the following morning, a newspaper printed the first part, and, a few hours later, the second part of the famous Prévotelle report, in which the problem was attacked in so masterly a fashion and solved with so profoundly impressive a display of method and logic. I shall never forget it. I shall never forget that, during that night, while I sat in my bedroom reflecting upon the manner in which Massignac had been spirited away, during that night when the long-expected thunderstorm burst over the Paris district, Benjamin Prévotelle was writing the opening pages of his report. And I shall never forget that I was on the point of hearing of all this from Benjamin Prévotelle himself!

At ten o'clock, in fact, one of the neighbours living nearest to the lodge, from whose house my uncle or Bérangère had been in the habit of telephoning, sent word to say that he was connected with Paris and that I was asked to come to the telephone without losing a minute.

I went round in a very bad temper. I was worn out with fatigue. It was raining cats and dogs; and the night was so dark that I knocked against the trees and houses as I walked.

The moment I arrived, I took up the receiver. Some one at the other end addressed me in a trembling voice:

"M. Beaugrand ... M. Beaugrand ... Excuse me ... I have discovered ..."

I did not understand at first and asked who was speaking.

"My name will convey nothing to you," was the answer. "Benjamin Prévotelle. I'm not a person of any particular importance. I am an engineer by profession; I left the Central School two years ago."

I interrupted him:

"One moment, please, one moment.... Hullo! ... Are you there? ... Benjamin Prévotelle? But I know your name! ... Yes, I remember, I've seen it in my uncle's papers."

"Do you mean that? You've seen my name in Noël Dorgeroux's papers?"

"Yes, in the middle of a paper, without comment of any kind."

The speaker's excitement increased:

"Oh," he said, "can it be possible? If Noël Dorgeroux made a note of my name, it proves that he read a pamphlet of mine, a year ago, and that he believed in the explanation of which I am beginning to catch a glimpse to-day."

"What explanation?" I asked, somewhat impatiently.

"You'll understand, monsieur, you'll understand when you read my report."

"Your report?"

"A report which I am writing now, to-night.... Listen: I was present at both the exhibitions in the Yard and I have discovered...."

"Discovered what, hang it all?"

"The problem, monsieur, the solution of the problem."

"What!" I exclaimed. "You've discovered it?"

"Yes, monsieur. I may tell you it's a very simple problem, so simple that I am anxious to be first in the field. Imagine, if any one else were to publish the truth before me! So I rang up Meudon on the chance of getting you called to the telephone.... Oh, do listen to me, monsieur: you must believe me and help me...."

"Of course, of course," I replied, "but I don't quite see ..."

"Yes, yes," Benjamin Prévotelle implored, appealing to me, clinging to me, so to speak, in a despairing tone of voice. "You can do a great deal. I only want a few particulars...."

I confess that Benjamin Prévotelle's statements left me a little doubtful. However, I answered:

"If a few particulars can be of any use to you ..."

"Perhaps one alone will do," he said. "It's this. The wall with the screen was entirely rebuilt by your uncle, Noël Dorgeroux, was it not?"

"Yes."

"And this wall, as you have said and as every one had observed, forms a given angle with its lower part."

"Yes."

"On the other hand, according to your depositions, Noël Dorgeroux intended to have a second amphitheatre built in his garden and to use the back of the same wall as a screen. That's so, is it not?"

"Yes."

"Well, this is the particular which I want you to give me. Have you noticed whether the back of the wall forms the same angle with its lower part?"

"Yes, I've noticed that."

"In that case," said Benjamin Prévotelle, with a note of

increasing triumph in his voice, "the evidence is complete. Noël Dorgeroux and I are agreed. The pictures do not come from the wall itself. The cause lies elsewhere. I will prove it; and, if M. Massignac would show a little willingness to help ..."

"Théodore Massignac was kidnapped this evening," I remarked.

"Kidnapped? What do you mean?"

I repeated:

"Yes, kidnapped; and I presume that the amphitheatre will be closed until further notice."

"But this is terrible, it's awful!" gasped Benjamin Prévotelle. "Why, in that case they couldn't verify my theory! There would never be any more pictures! No, look here, it's impossible. Just think, I don't know the indispensable formula! Nobody does, except Massignac. Oh, no, it is absolutely necessary ... Hullo, hullo! Don't cut me off, mademoiselle! ... One moment more, monsieur. I'll tell you the whole truth about the pictures. Three or four words will be enough.... Hullo, hullo! ..."

Benjamin Prévotelle's voice suddenly died away. I was clearly aware of the insuperable distance that separated him from me at the very moment when I was about to learn the miraculous truth which he in his turn laid claim to have discovered.

I waited anxiously. A few minutes passed. Twice the telephone-bell rang without my receiving any call. I decided to go away and had reached the bottom of the stairs when I was summoned back in a hurry. Some one was asking for me on the wire.

"Some one!" I said, going upstairs again. "But it must be the same person."

And I at once took up the receiver:

"Are you there? Is that M. Prévotelle?"

At first I heard only my name, uttered in a very faint, indistinct voice, a woman's voice:

"Victorien.... Victorien...."

"Hullo!" I cried, very excitedly, though I did not yet understand. "Hullo! ... Yes, it's I, Victorien Beaugrand. I happened to be at the telephone.... Hullo! ... Who is it speaking?"

For a few seconds the voice sounded nearer and then seemed to fall away. After that came perfect silence. But I had caught these few words:

"Help, Victorien! ... My father's life is in danger: help! ... Come to the Blue Lion at Bougival...."

I stood dumbfounded. I had recognised Bérangère's voice:

"Bérangère," I muttered, "calling on me for help...."

Without even pausing to think, I rushed to the station.

A train took me to Saint-Cloud and another two stations

further. Wading through the mud, under the pelting rain, and losing my way in the dark, I covered the mile or two to Bougival on foot, arriving in the middle of the night. The Blue Lion was closed. But a small boy dozing under the porch asked me if I was M. Victorien Beaugrand. When I answered that I was, he said that a lady, by the name of Bérangère, had told him to wait for me and take me to her, at whatever time I might arrive.

I trudged beside the boy, through the empty streets of the little town, to the banks of the Seine, which we followed for some distance. The rain had stopped, but the darkness was still impenetrable.

"The boat is here," said the boy.

"Oh, are we crossing?"

"Yes, the young lady is hiding on the other side. Be very careful not to make a noise."

We landed soon after. Then a stony path took us to a house where the boy gave three knocks on the door.

Some one opened the door. Still following my guide, I went up a few steps, crossed a passage lighted by a candle and was shown into a dark room with some one waiting in it. Instantly the light of an electric lamp struck me full in the face.

The barrel of a revolver was pointed at me and a man's voice said:

"Silence, do you understand? The least sound, the least attempt at escape; and you're done for. Otherwise you have nothing to fear; and the best thing you can do is to go to sleep."

The door was closed behind me. Two bolts were shot.

I had fallen into the trap which the man Velmot—I did not hesitate to fix upon him at once—had laid for me through the instrumentality of Bérangère.

This unaccountable adventure, like all those in which Bérangère was involved, did not alarm me unduly at the moment. I was no doubt too weary to seek reasons for the conduct of the girl and of the man under whose instructions she was acting. Why had she betrayed me? How had I incurred the man Velmot's ill-will? And what had induced him to imprison me, if I had nothing to fear from him as he maintained? These were all idle questions. After groping through the room and finding that it contained a bed, or rather a mattress and blankets, I took off my boots and outer clothing, wrapped myself in the blankets and in a few minutes was fast asleep.

I slept well into the following day. Meanwhile some one must have entered the room, for I saw on a table a hunk of new bread and a bottle of water. The cell which I occupied was a small one. Enough light to enable me to see came through the slats of a wooden shutter, which was firmly barricaded outside, as I discovered after opening the narrow window. One of the slats was half broken. Through the gap I perceived that my prison overlooked from a height of three or four feet a strip of ground at the edge of which little waves lapped among the reeds. Finding that, after crossing one river, I was facing another, I concluded that Velmot had brought me to an island in the Seine. Was this not the island which I had beheld, in a fleeting vision, on the chapel in the cemetery? And was it not here that Velmot and Massignac had established their head-quarters last winter?

Part of the day passed in silence. But, about five o'clock, I heard a sound of voices and outbursts of argument. This happened under my room and consequently in a cellar the grating of which opened beneath my window. On listening attentively, I seemed on several occasions to recognize Massignac's voice.

The discussion lasted fully an hour. Then some one made his appearance outside my window and called out:

"Hi, you chaps, come on and get ready! .... He's a stubborn beast and won't speak unless we make him."

It was the tall fellow who, the day before, had forced his way through the crowd in the Yard by making an outcry about a wounded man. It was Velmot, a leaner Velmot, without beard or glasses, Velmot, the coxcomb, the object of Bérangère's affections.

"I'll make him, the brute! Think of it. I've got him here, at my mercy: is it likely that I shouldn't be able to make him spew up his secret? No, no, we must finish it and by nightfall. You're still decided?"

He received two growls in reply. He sneered:

"He's not half badly trussed up, eh? All right. I'll do without you. Only just lend me a hand to begin with."

He stepped into a boat fastened to a ring on the bank. One of the men pushed it with a boat-hook between two stakes planted in the mud and standing out well above the reeds. Velmot knotted one end of a thick rope to the top of each stake and in the middle fastened an iron hook, which thus hung four or five feet above the water.

"That's it," he said, on returning. "I shan't want you any more. Take the other boat and go and wait for me in the garage. I'll join you there in three or four hours, when Massignac has blabbed his little story and after I've had a little plain speaking with our new prisoner. And then we'll be off."

He walked away with his two assistants. When I saw him again, twenty minutes later, he had a newspaper in his hand. He laid it on

93

a little table which stood just outside my window. Then he sat down and lit a cigar. He turned his back to me, hiding the table from my view. But at one moment he moved and I caught sight of his paper, the Journal du Soir, which was folded across the page and which bore a heading in capitals running right across the width of the sheet, with this sensational title:

"THE TRUTH ABOUT THE MEUDON

APPARITIONS REVEALED"

I was shaken to the very depths of my being. So the young student had not lied! Benjamin Prévotelle had discovered the truth and had managed, in the space of a few hours, to set it forth in the report of which he had spoken and to make it public.

Glued to the shutter, how I strove to read the opening lines of the article! These were the only lines that met my eyes, because of the manner in which the paper was folded. And how great was my excitement at each word that I made out!

I have carefully preserved a copy of that paper, by which a part at least of the great mystery was made known to me. Before reprinting the famous report, which Benjamin Prévotelle had published that morning, it said:

> "Yes, the fantastic problem is solved. A contemporary published this morning, in the form of 'An Open Letter to the Academy of Science,' the most sober, luminous and convincing report conceivable. We do not know whether the official experts will agree with the conclusions of the report, but we doubt if the objections, which for that matter are frankly stated by the author, are strong enough, however grave they may be, to demolish the theory which he propounds. The arguments seem unanswerable. The proofs are such as to compel belief. And what doubles the value of this admirable theory is that it does not merely appear to be unassailable, but opens up to us the widest and most marvellous horizons. In fact, Noël Dorgeroux's discovery is no longer limited to what it is or what it seems to be. It implies consequences which cannot be foretold. It is calculated to upset all our ideas of man's past and all our conceptions of his future. Not since the beginning of the world has there been an event to compare with this. It is at the same time the most incomprehensible event and the most natural, the most complex and the simplest. A great

scientist might have announced it to the world as the result of meditation. And he who, thanks both to able intuition and intelligent observation has achieved this inestimable glory is little more than a boy in years.

"We subjoin a few particulars gleaned in the course of an interview which Benjamin Prévotelle was good enough to grant us. We apologize for being able to give no more details concerning his personality. How should it be otherwise: Benjamin Prévotelle is twenty-three years of age. He..."

I had to stop here, as the subsequent lines escaped my eyes. Was I to learn more?

Velmot had risen from his chair and was walking to and fro. After a brief disappearance, he returned with a bottle of some liqueur, of which he drank two glasses in quick succession. Then he unfolded the newspaper and began to peruse the report or rather to reperuse it, for I had no doubt that he had read it before.

His chair was right against my shutter. He sat leaning back, so that I was able to see, not the end of the preliminary article, but the report itself, which he read rather slowly.

The daylight, proceeding from a sky whose clouds must have hidden the sun, was meantime diminishing. I read simultaneously with Velmot:

"An Open Letter to the Academy of Science

"I will beg you, gentlemen, to regard this memorandum as only the briefest possible introduction to the more important essay which I propose to write and to the innumerable volumes to which it is certain to give rise in every country, to which volumes also it will serve as a modest preface.

"I am writing hurriedly, allowing my pen to run away with me, improvising hastily as I go along. You will find omissions and defects which I do not attempt to conceal and which are due in equal proportions to the restricted number of observations which we were able to make at Meudon and to the obstinate refusal which M. Théodore Massignac opposes to every request for additional information. But the remarkable feeling aroused by the miraculous pictures makes it my duty to offer the results, as yet extremely incomplete, of an investigation in respect of which I have the legitimate ambition to reserve the right of priority. I thus hope, by confining my hypotheses to a definite channel, to assist towards establishing the truth and relieving the public mind.

"My investigations were commenced immediately after the first revelations made by M. Victorien Beaugrand. I collated all his statements. I analysed all his impressions. I seized upon all that Noël Dorgeroux had said. I went over the details of all his experiments. And in consequence of carefully weighing and examining all these things I did not come to the first performance at Meudon with my hands in my pockets, as a lover of sensations and a dabbler in mystery. On the contrary, I came with a well-considered plan and with a few working-implements, deliberately selected and concealed under my own clothing and that of some of my friends who were good enough to assist me.

"First of all, a camera. This was a matter of some difficulty. M. Théodore Massignac had his misgivings and had prohibited the introduction of so much as the smallest Kodak. Nevertheless I succeeded. I had to. I had to provide a definite answer to a first question, which might be called the critical question: are the Meudon apparitions due to individual or collective suggestions, possessing no reality outside those who experience them, or have they a real and external cause? That answer may certainly be deduced from the absolute identity of the impressions received by all the spectators. But to-day I am adducing a direct proof which I consider to be unassailable. The camera refuses any sort of suggestion. The camera is not a brain in which the picture can create itself, in which an hallucination is formed out of internal data. It is a witness that does not lie and is not mistaken. Well, this witness has spoken. The sensitive plate certifies the phenomena to be real. I hold at the disposal of the Academy seven negatives of the screen thus obtained by instantaneous exposures. Two of them, representing Rheims Cathedral on fire, are remarkably clear.

"Here then the first point is settled: the screen is the seat of an emanation of light-rays.

"While I was obtaining the proofs of this emanation, I submitted it to the means of investigation which physics places at our disposal. I was not, unfortunately, able to make as many or as accurate experiments as I should have wished. The distance of the wall, the local arrangements and the inadequacy of the light emitted by the screen were against me. Nevertheless, by using the spectroscope and the polarimeter, I ascertained that this light did not appear to differ perceptibly from the natural light diffused by a white surface.

"But a more tangible result and one to which I attach the greatest importance was obtained by examining the screen by means of a revolving mirror. It is well known that, if our ordinary cinematographic pictures projected on a screen be viewed in a mirror to which we impart a rapid rotary movement, the successive pictures are dislocated and yield images in the field of the mirror. A similar effect can be obtained, though less distinctly, by turning one's head quickly so as to project the successive pictures upon different points of the retina. It was therefore indicated that I should apply this method of analysis to the animated projections produced at Meudon. I was thus able to prove positively that these projections, like those of the ordinary cinematograph, break up into separate and successive images, but with a rapidity which is notably greater than in the operations to which we are accustomed, for I found that they average 28 to the second. On the other hand, these images are not emitted at regular intervals. I observed rhythmical alterations of acceleration and retardation and I am inclined to believe that the rhythmical variations are not unconnected with the extraordinary impression of steroscopic relief which all the spectators at Meudon received.

"The foregoing observations led up to a scientific certainty and naturally guided my investigations into a definite channel: the Meudon pictures are genuine cinematographic projections thrown upon the screen and perceived by the spectators in the ordinary manner. But where is the projecting-apparatus? How does it work? This is where the gravest difficulty lies, for hitherto no trace of an apparatus has been discovered, nor even the least clue to the existence of any apparatus whatever.

"Is it allowable to suppose, as I did not fail to do, that the projections may proceed from within the screen, by means of an underground device which it is not impossible to imagine? This last theory would obviously greatly relieve our minds, by attributing the visions to some clever trick. But it was not without good reason that first M. Victorien Beaugrand and afterwards the audience itself refused to accept it. The visions bear a stamp of authenticity and unexpectedness which strikes all who see them, without any exception. Moreover, the specialists in cinematographic "faking," when questioned, frankly proclaim that their expert knowledge is at a loss and their technique at fault. It may even be declared that the exhibitor of these images possesses no power beyond that of receiving them on a suitable screen and that he himself does not know what is about to appear on the screen. Lastly, it may be added that the preparation of such films as that would be a long and complicated operation, necessitating an extensive equipment and a numerous staff of actors; and it is really impossible that these preparations can have been effected in absolute secrecy.

"This is exactly the point to which my enquiries had led me on the night before the last, after the first performance. I will not presume to say that I knew more than any chance member of the public about that which constitutes the fundamental nature of the problem. Nevertheless, when I took my seat at the second performance, I was in a better condition mentally than any of the other onlookers. I was standing on solid ground. I was self controlled, free of feverish excitement or any other factor that might diminish the intensity of my attention. I was hampered by no preconceived ideas; and no new idea, no new fact could come within my grasp without my immediately perceiving it.

"This was what happened. The new fact was the bewildering and mystifying spectacle of the grotesque Shapes. I did not at once draw the conclusion which this spectacle entailed, or at least I was not aware of so doing. But my perceptions were aroused. Those beings equipped with three arms became connected in my mind with the initial riddle of the Three Eyes. If I did not yet understand, at least I had a presentiment of the truth; if I did not know, at least I suspected that I was about to know. The door was opening. The light was beginning to dawn.

"A few minutes later, as will be remembered, came the gruesome picture of a cart conveying two gendarmes, a priest and a king who was being led to his death. It was a confused, fragmentary, mutilated picture, continually broken up and pieced together again. Why? For, after all, the thing was not normal. Until then, as we know and as M. Victorien Beaugrand had told us, until then the pictures were always admirably distinct. And suddenly we beheld a flickering, defective image, confused, dim and at moments almost invisible. Why?

"At that critical instant, this was the only train of thought permissible. The horror and strangeness of the spectacle no longer counted. Why was this, technically speaking, a defective picture? Why was the faultless mechanism, which until now had worked with perfect smoothness, suddenly disordered? What was the grain of sand that had thrown it out of gear?

"Really the problem was proposed to me with a simplicity that confounded me. The terms of the problem were familiar to all. We had before us cinematographic pictures. These cinematographic pictures did not proceed from the wall itself. They did not come from any part of the amphitheatre. Then whence were they projected? And what obstacle was now preventing their free projection?

"Instinctively, I made the only movement that could be made, the movement which a child would have made if that elementary question had been put to it: I raised my eyes to the sky.

"It was absolutely clear, an immense, empty sky.

"Clear and empty, yes, but in the part which my eyes were able to interrogate. Was it the same in the part hidden from my view by the upper wall of the amphitheatre?

"The mere silent utterance of the words which propounded the question was enough to make me almost swoon with anxiety. They bore the tremendous truth within themselves. I had only to speak them for the great mystery to vanish utterly.

"With trembling limbs and a heart that almost ceased to beat, I climbed to the top of the amphitheatre and gazed at the horizon. Yonder, towards the west, light clouds were floating...."

CHAPTER XIV

MASSIGNAC AND VELMOT

"Clouds were floating.... Clouds were floating...."

These words of the report, which I repeated mechanically while trying to decipher what followed, were the last that I was able to read. Night was falling rapidly. My eyes, tired by the strain and difficulty of reading, strove in vain against the increasing darkness and suddenly refused to obey any further effort.

Besides, Velmot rose soon after and walked to the bank of the river. The time had come for action.

What that action was to be I did not ask. Since the beginning of my captivity, I had entertained no personal fears, even though Velmot had referred to an interview, accompanied by "a little plain-speaking," which he had in store for me. But the great secret of the Yard continued to possess my thoughts so much that nothing that happened had any effect upon me except in so far as it was useful or injurious to Noël Dorgeroux's cause. There was some one now who knew the truth; and the world was about to learn it. How could I trouble about anything else? How could anything interest me except Benjamin Prévotelle's accurate arguments, the ingenuity of his investigations and the important results which he had achieved?

Oh, how I too longed to know! What could the new theory be? Did it fit in with all the teaching of reality? And would it fully satisfy me, who, when all was said, had penetrated farther than any other into the heart of that reality and reaped the largest harvest of observations?

What astonished me was that I did not understand. And I am even more astonished now. Though standing on the very threshold of the sanctuary, the door of which was opened to me, I was unable to see. No light flashed upon me. What did Benjamin Prévotelle mean to say? What was the significance of those clouds drifting in a corner of the sky? If they tempered the light of the sunset and thus exerted an influence over the pictures of the screen, why did Benjamin Prévotelle ask me on the telephone about the surface of the wall which faced precisely the opposite quarter of the heavens, that is the east? And why did he accept my answer as confirming his theory?

Velmot's voice drew me from my dreams and brought me back to the window which I had left a few minutes earlier. He was stooping over the grating and sneering:

"Well, Massignac, are you ready for the operation? I'll get you out this way: that'll save my dragging you round by the stairs."

Velmot went down the stairs; and I soon heard beneath me the loud outburst of a renewed argument, ending in howls and then in a sudden silence which was the most impressive of all. I now received my first notion of the terrible scene which Velmot was preparing; and, without wasting my pity on the wretched Massignac, I shuddered at the thought that my turn might come next.

The thing was done as Velmot had said. Massignac, bandaged like a swathed mummy, rigid and gagged, rose slowly from the cellar. Velmot then returned, dragged him by the shoulders to the edge of the river and tipped him into the boat.

Then, standing on the bank, he addressed him as follows:

"Now, Massignac, my beauty, this is the third time that I'm appealing to your common sense; and I'll do it again presently, for the fourth time, if you force me to. But you're going to give in, I fancy. Come, think a moment. Think what you would do in my place. You'd act yourself as I am doing, wouldn't you? Then what are you waiting for? Why don't you speak? Does your gag bother you? Just nod your head and I'll move it. Do you agree? No? In that case you mustn't be surprised if we start upon the fourth and last phase of our conversation. All my apologies if it strikes you as still more unpleasant."

Velmot sat down beside his victim, wielded the boat-hook and pushed the boat between the two stakes projecting above the water.

These two stakes marked the boundaries of the field of vision which the gap in the shutter afforded me. The water played around them, spangled with sparks of light. The moon had appeared from behind the clouds; and I distinctly saw every detail of the "operation," to use Velmot's expression.

"Don't resist, Massignac," he said. "It won't help.... Eh? What? You think I'm too rough, do you? My lord's made of glass, is he? Now then! Yoop! Is that right? Capital!"

He had stood Massignac up against himself and placed his left arm round him. With his right hand he took hold of the iron hook fastened to the rope between the two stakes, pulled it down and inserted the point under the bonds with which Massignac was swathed, at the height of the shoulders.

"Capital!" he repeated. "You see, I needn't trouble to hold you. You're standing up all by yourself, my boy, like a monkey on a stick."

He took the boat-hook again, hooked it into the stones on the bank and made the boat glide from under Massignac's body, which

101

promptly sank. The rope had sagged. Only half of his body emerged above the water.

And Velmot said to his former confederate, in a low voice, which I could hear, however, without straining my ears. I have always believed that Velmot spoke that day with the intention that I should hear—:

"This is what I had in mind, old chap; and we haven't much more to say to each other. Remember, in an hour from now, possibly sooner, the water will be above your mouth, which won't make it very easy for you to speak. And of that hour I ought in decency to give you fifty minutes for reflection."

He splashed a little water over Massignac's head with the boat-hook. Then he continued, with a laugh:

"You quite grasp the position, don't you? The rope by which you're fastened, like an ox in a stall, is fixed to the two stakes by a couple of slip-knots, nothing more ... so that, at the least movement, the knots slip down an inch or so. You will have noticed it just now, when I let you go. Blinkety blump! You went down a half a head lower! Besides that, the weight alone of your body is enough.... You're slipping, old fellow, you're slipping all the time; and nothing can stop you ... unless, of course, you speak. Are you ready to speak?"

The moonbeams shifted to and fro, casting light or shade upon the horrible scenes. I could see the black shape of Massignac, who himself always remained in semidarkness. The water came half-way up his chest.

Velmot continued:

"Logically, old fellow, you're bound to speak. The position is so clear. We plotted between us a little piece of business which succeeded, thanks to our joint efforts; but you have pocketed all the profits, thanks to your trickery. I want my share, that's all. And for this you need do no more than tell me Noël Dorgeroux's famous formula and supply me with the means of making the experiment to begin with. After that I'll give you back your liberty for I shall feel certain that you will allow me my share of the profits, for fear of competition. Is it a bargain?"

Théodore Massignac must have made a gesture of denial or uttered a grunt of refusal, for he received a smack across the face which resounded through the silence.

"I'm sure you'll excuse me, old fellow," said Velmot, "but you'd try the patience of a plaster saint! Do you really mean to say that you would rather croak? Or perhaps you think I intend to give in? Or that some one will come and help you out of your mess? You ass! You chose this place yourself last winter! No boats come this way.

Opposite, nothing but fields. So there's no question of a rescue. Nor of pity either! Why, hang it all, don't you realize the positions? And yet I showed you the article in this morning's paper. With the exception of the formula, it's all set out there: all Dorgeroux's secret and all yours! So who's to tell us that they won't quite easily find the formula? Who's to tell us that, in a fortnight, in a week, the whole thing won't be given away and that I shall have had my hands on a million of money, like a fool, without grabbing it? Oh, no, that would never do!"

There was a pause. A ray of light gave me a glimpse of Massignac. The water had risen above his shoulders.

"I've nothing more to say to you," said Velmot. "We'll make an end of it. Do you refuse?"

He waited for a moment and continued:

"In that case, since you refuse, I won't insist: what's the good? You shall decide your own fate and take the final plunge. Good-bye, old man. I'm going to drink a glass and smoke a pipe to your health."

He bent towards his victim and added:

"Still, it's a chap's duty to provide for everything. If, by chance you think better of it, if you have an inspiration at the last moment, you have only to call me, quite softly.... There, I'm loosening your gag a bit.... Good-bye, Théodore."

Velmot pushed the boat back and landed, grumbling:

"It's a dog's life! What a fool the brute is!"

As arranged, he sat down again, after bringing the chair and table to the water's edge, poured himself out a glass of liqueur and lit his pipe:

"Here's to your good health, Massignac," he said. "At the present rate, I can see that, in twenty minutes from now, you'll be having a drink too. Whatever you do, don't forget to call me. I'm listening for all I'm worth, old chum."

The moon had become veiled with clouds, which must have been very dense, for the bank grew so dark that I could hardly distinguish Velmot's figure. As a matter of fact, I was persuaded that the implacable contest would end in some compromise and that Velmot would give way or Massignac speak. Nevertheless, ten or perhaps fifteen minutes passed, minutes which seemed to me interminable. Velmot smoked quietly and Massignac gave a series of little whimpers, but did not call out. Five minutes more. Velmot rose angrily:

"It's no use whining, you blasted fool! I've had enough of messing about. Will you speak? No? Then die, you scamp!"

And I heard him snarling between his teeth:

"Perhaps I shall manage better with the other one."

Whom did he mean by "the other one" ? Me?

In point of fact, he turned to the left, that is towards the part of the house where the door was:

"Damn it!" he swore, almost immediately.

There was an ejaculation. And then I heard nothing more from that direction.

What had happened? Had Velmot knocked against the wall, in the dark, or against an open shutter?

I could not see him from where I stood. The table and chair were faintly outlined in the gloom. Beyond was the pitchy darkness from which came Massignac's muffled whimper.

"Velmot is on his way," I said to myself. "A few seconds more and he will be here."

The reason for his coming I did not understand, any more than the reason for trepanning me. Did he think that I knew the formula and that I had refrained from denouncing Massignac because of an understanding between him and myself? In that case, did he mean to compel me to speak, by employing with me the same methods as with his former accomplice? Or was it a question of Bérangère between us, of the Bérangère whom we both loved and whose name, to my surprise, he had not even mentioned to Massignac? These were so many problems to which he would provide the reply:

"That is," I thought, "if he comes."

For, after all, he was not there; and there was not a sound in the house. What was he doing? For some little while I stood with my ear glued to the door by which he should have entered, ready to defend myself though unarmed.

He did not come.

I went back to the window. There was no sound on that side either.

And the silence was terrible, that silence which seemed to increase and to spread all over the river and into space, that silence which was no longer broken even by Massignac's stifled moaning.

In vain I tried to force my eyes to see. The water of the river remained invisible. I no longer saw and I no longer heard Théodore Massignac.

I could no longer see him and I could no longer hear him. It was a terrifying reflection! Had he slipped down? Had the deadly, suffocating water risen to his mouth and nostrils?

I struck the shutter with a mighty blow of my fist. The thought that Massignac was dead or about to die, that thought which until then I had not realised very clearly, filled me with dismay. Massignac's death meant the definite and irreparable loss of the secret. Massignac's death meant that Noël Dorgeroux was dying for the second time.

I redoubled my efforts. There was certainly no doubt in my mind that Velmot was at hand and that he and I would have to fight it out; but I did not care about that. No consideration could stop me. I had then and there to hasten to the assistance not of Massignac, but as it appeared to me, of Noël Dorgeroux, whose wonderful work was about to be destroyed. All that I had done hitherto, in protecting by my silence, Théodore Massignac's criminal enterprise, I was bound to continue by saving from death the man who knew the indispensable formula.

As my fists were not enough, I broke a chair and used it to hammer one of the bars. Moreover, the shutter was not very strong, as some of the slats were already partly missing. Another split and yet another. I was able to slip my arm through and to lift an iron cross-bar hinged to the outside. The shutter gave way at once. I had only to step over the window-sill and drop to the ground below.

Velmot was certainly leaving the field clear for me.

Without losing an instant, I passed by the chair, threw over the table and easily found the boat:

"I'm here!" I shouted to Massignac. "Hold on!"

With a strong push I reached one of the stakes, repeating:

"Hold on! Hold on! I'm here!"

I seized the rope in both hands, at the level of the water, and felt for the hook, expecting to strike against Massignac's head.

I touched nothing. The rope had slipped down; the hook was in the water and carried no weight. The body must have gone to the bottom; and the current had swept it away.

Nevertheless, on the off-chance, I dipped my hand as far as I could into the water. But a shot suddenly pulled me up short. A bullet had whistled past my ear. At the same time, Velmot, whom I could just make out crouching on the bank, like a man dragging himself on all fours, stuttered, in a choking voice:

"Oh, you scum, you took your opportunity, did you? And you think perhaps you're going to save Massignac? Just you wait a bit, you blighter!"

He fired two more shots, guessing at my whereabouts, for I was sculling away rapidly. Neither of them touched me. Soon I was out of range.

CHAPTER XV

THE SPLENDID THEORY

It is not only to-day, when I am relating that tragic scene, that it appears to me in the light of a subsidiary episode to my story. I already had that impression at the time when it was being enacted. My reason for laying no greater stress on my alarm and on the horror of certain facts is that all this was to me only an interlude. Massignac's sufferings and his disappearance and Velmot's inexplicable behaviour, in abandoning for some minutes the conduct of a matter to which he had until then applied himself with such diabolical eagerness, were just so many details which became blotted out by the tremendous events represented by Benjamin Prévotelle's discovery.

And to such an extent was this event the central point of all my preoccupations that the idea had occurred to me, as I rushed to Massignac's assistance, of snatching from the chair the newspaper in which I had read the first half of the essay! To be free meant above all things—even above saving Massignac and, through him, the formula—the opportunity of reading the rest of the essay and of learning what the whole world must already have learnt!

I made the circuit of the island in my boat and, shaping my course by certain lights, ran her ashore on the main bank. A tram went by. Some of the shops were open. I was between Bougival and Port-Marly.

At ten o'clock in the evening I was sitting in a bedroom in a Paris hotel and unfolding a newspaper. But I had not had the patience to wait so long. On the way, by the feeble lights of the tram-car, I glanced at a few lines of the article. One word told me everything. I too was acquainted with Benjamin Prévotelle's marvellous theory. I knew and, knowing, I believed.

The reader will recall the place which I had reached in my uncomfortable perusal of the report. Benjamin Prévotelle's studies and experiments had led him to conclude, first, that the Meudon pictures were real cinematographic projections and, next, that these projections, since they came from no part of the amphitheatre, must come from some point more remote. Now the last picture, that representing the revolutionary doings of the 21st January, was hampered by some obstacle. What obstacle? His mental condition being what it was, what could Benjamin Prévotelle do other than raise his eyes to the sky?

The sky was clear. Was it also clear beyond the part that could be observed from the lower benches of the amphitheatre? Benjamin Prévotelle climbed to the top and looked at the horizon.

Yonder, towards the west, clouds were floating.

And Benjamin Prévotelle continued, repeating his phrase:

"Clouds were floating! And, because of the fact that clouds were floating on the horizon, the pictures on the screen grew less distinct or even vanished altogether. It may be said that this was a coincidence. On three separate occasions, when the film lost its brilliancy, I turned towards the horizon: on each occasion clouds were passing. Could three coincidences of this kind be due to chance? Can any scientific mind fail to see herein a relation of cause and effect or to admit that, in this instance, as in that of many visions previously observed, which were disturbed by an unknown cause, the interposition of the clouds acted as a veil by intercepting the projection on its way? I was not able to make a fourth test. But that did not matter. I had now advanced so far that I was able to work and reflect without being stopped by any obstacle. There is no such thing as being checked mid-way in our pursuit of certain truths. Once we catch a glimpse of them, they become revealed in their entirety.

"At first, to be sure, scientific logic, instead of referring the explanation which I was so eagerly seeking to the data of human science, flung me, almost despite myself, into an ever more mysterious region. And, when, after this second display, I returned home—this was three hours ago at most—I asked myself whether it would not be better to confess my ignorance than to go rushing after theories which suddenly seemed to me to lie beyond the confines of science. But how could I have done so? Despite myself I continued to work at the problem, to imagine. Induction fitted into deduction. Proofs were accumulating. Even as I was hesitating to enter upon a path whose direction confounded me, I reached the goal and found myself sitting down to a table, pen in hand, to write a report which was dictated by my reason as much as by my imagination.

"Thus the first step was taken: in obedience to the imperious summons of reality, I admitted the theory of extra-terrestrial communications, or at least of communications coming from beyond the clouds. Was I to think that they emanated from some airship hovering in the sky, beyond that cloud-belt? Leaving aside the fact that no such airship was ever observed, we must remark that luminous projections powerful enough to light the screen at Meudon from a distance of several miles would leave in the air a trail of diffused light which could not escape notice. Lastly, in the present condition of science, we are at liberty to declare positively that such projections would be quite incapable of realization.

"What then? Were we to cast our eyes farther, traverse space at one bound and assume that the projections have an origin which is not only extraterrestrial but extrahuman?

"Now the great word is written. The idea is no longer my property. How will it be received by those to whom this report will reveal it to-morrow? Will they welcome it with the same fervour and the same awe-struck emotion that thrilled me, with the distrust at the beginning and the same final enthusiasm?

"Let us, if you will, recover our composure. The examination of the phenomena has led us to a very definite conclusion. However startling this conclusion be, let us examine it also, with perfect detachment, and try to subject it to all the tests which we are able to impose upon it.

"Extrahuman projections: what does that mean? The expression seems vague; and our thoughts wander at random. Let us look into the matter more closely. Let us first of all establish as an impassable boundary the frontiers of our solar system and, in this immense circle, concentrate our gaze upon the more accessible and consequently the nearer points. For, when all is said, if there be really projections, they must necessarily, whether extrahuman or human, emanate from fixed points, situated in space. They must therefore emanate from those luminaries within sight of the earth to which, in the last report, we have some right to attribute the origin of those projections. I consider that there are five such fixed points: the moon, the sun, Jupiter, Mars and Venus.

"If, furthermore, we suppose as the more likely theory that the projections follow a rectilinear direction, then the unknown luminary from which the apparitions emanate will have to satisfy two conditions: first, it must be in such a position that photographs can be taken from it; secondly, it must be in such a position that the images obtained can be transmitted to us. Let us take as an instance a case in which it is possible to fix the place and date. The first Montgolfier balloon, filled with hot air, was sent up from Annonay at four o'clock in the afternoon on the 5th of June, 1783. It is easy, by referring to the contemporary calendars, to learn which celestial bodies were at that moment above the horizon and at what height. We thus find that Mars, Jupiter and the moon were invisible, whereas the sun and Venus were at 50 and 23 degrees respectively above the horizon of Annonay and, of course, towards the west. These two luminaries alone then were in a position to witness the experiment of the brothers Montgolfier. But they did not witness it from the same altitude: a view taken from the sun would have shown things as seen from above, whereas, at the same hour, Venus would have shown then from an angle very nearly approaching the horizontal.

"This is a first clue. Are we able to check it? Yes, by turning up the date on which the projections of the view then secured as observed by Victorien Beaugrand and by determining whether, on that date, the projecting luminary was able to light up the screen at Meudon. Well, on that day, at the hour which Victorien Beaugrand has given us, Mars and the moon were invisible, Jupiter was in the east, the sun close to the horizon and Venus a little way above it. Projections emanating from the last-named planet could therefore have fallen upon the screen, which as we know faced westwards.

"This example shows us that, however frail my theory may appear, we are now able and shall be even better able in the future to subject it to a strict control. I did not fail to resort to this method in respect of the other pictures, and I will give in a special table, appended to this essay, a list of the data which I have verified, a list necessarily drawn up, in some haste. Well, in all the cases which I examined, the views were taken and projected under such conditions that they can logically be referred to the planet Venus and to that planet alone.

"Yet again, two of these views, that which revealed to Victorien Beaugrand and his uncle the execution of Miss Cavell and that which enabled us to witness the bombardment of Rheims, seem to have been taken, the first in the morning, because Miss Cavell was executed in the morning, and the second from the east, because it showed a shell fired at a statue which stood on the east front of the cathedral. This proves that the views could be taken indifferently in the morning or the evening, from the west or the east; and it is surely a powerful argument in favour of my theory, because Venus, which is both the Evening and the Morning Star, faces the earth at daybreak from the east and at sunset from the west and because Noël Dorgeroux (as M. Victorien Beaugrand has just confirmed to me by telephone), because Noël Dorgeroux, that magnificent visionary, had had his wall constructed with two surfaces having an identical inclination towards the sky, one facing west, the other east and each in turn exposed to the rays of Venus the Evening Star and Venus the Morning Star!

"These are the proofs which I am able to furnish for the time being. There are others. There is for instance the time of the apparitions. Venus is sinking towards the horizon; on the earth twilight reigns; and the pictures can be formed regardless of the sunlight. Remark also that Noël Dorgeroux, deferring all his experiments, last winter altered the whole arrangement of the Yard and demolished the old garden. Now this break coincides exactly with a period during which the position of Venus on the farther side of the sun prevented it from communicating with the earth. All these proofs will be reinforced by a more exhaustive essay and by an analytical examination of the pictures that have been or will be shown to us.

"But though I have written this report without stopping to answer the objections and difficulties which arise at every line, though I have been contented myself with setting forth the logical and almost inevitable sequence of the deductions which led up to my theory. I should be failing in respect to the academy and to the public if I allowed it to be believed that I am not fully conscious of the weight of those objections and difficulties. I did not, however, consider this a reason for abandoning my task. Though it be our duty to bow when science utters a formal veto, on the other hand duty orders us to persist when science is content merely to confess its ignorance. This is the twofold principle which I observed in seeking no longer the source of the projections, but rather the manner in which they were able to appear, for that is where the whole problem lies. It is easy to declare that they emanate from Venus; it is not easy to explain how they travel through space and how they exercise their action, at a distance of many millions of miles, on an imperceptible screen with a surface of three or four hundred square feet. I am confronted with physical laws which I am not entitled to transgress. I am entitled at most to advance where science is obliged to be mute.

"Therefore and without any sort of discussion I admit that we are debarred from supposing that light can be the agent of the transmissions which have been observed. The laws of diffraction indeed are absolutely opposed to the strictly rectilinear propagation of luminous rays and hence to the formation and reception of pictures at the exceptional distances actually under consideration. Not only are the laws of geometrical optics merely a somewhat rough approximation, but the complicated refractions which would inevitably occur in the atmospheres of the earth and Venus would disturb the optical images. The veto of science therefore is peremptory in so far as the possibility of these optical transmissions is concerned.

"For that matter, I should be quite willing to believe that the inhabitants of Venus have already tried to correspond with us through the intermediary of luminous signals and that, if they abandoned their endeavours, this was precisely because the imperfection of our human science made them useless. We know in fact that Lowell and Schiaparelli saw on the face of Venus brilliant specks and a transient gleam which they themselves attributed either to volcanic eruptions or, as is more probable, to the attempts at communication of which I have spoken.

"But science does not prevent us from asking ourselves whether, after the failure of these attempts, the inhabitants of Venus did not resort to another method of correspondence. How can we avoid thinking, for instance, of the X-rays, whose strictly rectilinear path would allow of the formation of pictures so clear that one could wish for nothing better? In fact it is not impossible that these rays are employed for the emission received on the Meudon screen, though the quality of the light when analyzed in the spectroscope makes the supposition highly improbable. But how are we to explain by means of X-rays the taking of the terrestrial views of which we saw the moving outline on the screen? We know, of course, if we go back to the concrete example to which I referred just now, we know that neither the brothers Montgolfier nor the surrounding landscape emitted X-rays. It is not therefore through the medium of these rays that the Venusians can have secured the instantaneous photographs which they afterwards transmitted to us.

"Well, this exhausts all the possibilities of an explanation which can be referred to the present data of science. I declare positively that to-day, in this essay, I should not have dared to venture into the domain of theory and to suggest a solution in which my own labours are involved, if Noël Dorgeroux had not in a manner authorized me to do so. The fact is that, twelve months ago, I issued a pamphlet, entitled An Essay on Universal Gravitation, which fell flat on publication, but which must have attracted Noël Dorgeroux's particular attention, because his nephew, Victorien Beaugrand, found my name written among his papers and because Noël Dorgeroux cannot have known my name except through this pamphlet. Nor would he have taken the trouble to write it down, if the theory of the rays of gravitation which I developed in my pamphlet had not appeared to him to be exactly adapted to the problem raised by his discovery?

"I will therefore ask the reader to refer to my pamphlet. He will there find the results, vague but by no means negligible, which I was able to explain by my experiments with this radiation. He will see that it is propagated in a strictly rectilinear direction and with a speed which is thrice that of light, so that it would not take more than 46 seconds to reach Venus at the time when she is nearest to the earth. He will see lastly that, though the existence of these rays, thanks to which universal attraction is exercised according to the Newtonian laws, is not yet admitted and though I have not yet succeeded in making them visible by means of suitable receivers, I nevertheless give proofs of their existence which must be taken into consideration. And Noël Dorgeroux's approval also is a proof that they must not be neglected.

"On the other hand, we have the right to believe that, while our poor rudimentary science may, after centuries and centuries of efforts, have remained ignorant of the essential factor of the equilibrium of the planets, the Venusian scientists long since passed this inferior stage of knowledge and that they possess photographic receivers which allow films to be taken by means of the rays of gravitation and this by methods of truly wonderful perfection. They were therefore waiting. Looking down upon our planet, knowing all that happened here, witnessing our helplessness, they were waiting to communicate with us by the only means that appeared to them possible. They were waiting, patiently and persistently, formidably equipped, sweeping our soil with the invisible sheaves of rays assembled in their projectors and receivers, searching and prying into every nook and corner.

"And one day the wonderful thing happened. One day the shaft of rays struck the layer of substance on the screen where and where alone the spontaneous work of chemical decomposition and immediate reconstitution could be performed. On that day, thanks to Noël Dorgeroux and thanks to luck, as we must confess, for Noël Dorgeroux was pursuing an entirely different series of experiments on that particular day, the Venusians established the connection between the two planets. The greatest fact in the history of the world was accomplished.

"There is evidence even that the Venusians knew of Noël Dorgeroux's earlier experiments, that they realized their importance, that they interested themselves in his labours and that they followed the events of his life, for it is now many years since they took the pictures showing how his son Dominique was killed in the war. But I will not recapitulate in detail each of the films displayed at Meudon. This is a work which anybody can now perform in the light of the theory which I am setting forth. But we must consider attentively the process by which the Venusians tried to give those films a sort of uniformity. It has been rightly said that the sign of the Three Eyes is a trade-mark, like the mark of any of our great cinematograph-producers, a trade-mark also very strikingly proves the superhuman resources possessed by the Venusians, since they succeed in giving to those Three Eyes, which have no relation to our human eyes, not only the expression of our eyes but something much more impressive, the expression of the eyes of the person destined to be the principal character in the film.

"But why was this particular mark chosen? Why eyes and why three? At the stage which we have now reached, need we answer this question? The Venusians themselves have furnished the reply by showing us that apparently absurd film in which Shapes assuredly lived and moved in our sight in accordance with the lines and principle of

Venusian life. Were we not the breathless spectators of a picture taken among them and from them? Did we not behold, to make a companion picture to the death of Louis XVI, an incident representing the martyrdom of some great personage whom the executioners tore to pieces with their three hands, severing from his body a sort of shapeless head provided with three eyes?

"Three Hands! Three Eyes! Dare I, on the strength of this fragile basis, go beyond what we saw and declare that the Venusian possesses the complete symmetry of the triangle, just as man, with his two eyes, his two ears and his two arms, possesses bilateral symmetry? Shall I try to explain his method of progressing by successive distentions and of moving vertically along vertical streets, in towns built perpendicularly? Shall I have the courage to state, as I believe, that he is provided with organs which give him a magnetic sense, a sense of space, an electric sense and so on, organs numbered by threes? No. These are details with which the Venusian scientists will supply us on the day when it pleases them to enter into correspondence with us.

"And, believe me, they will not fail to do so. All their efforts for centuries past have been directed towards this object. 'Let us talk,' they will say to us soon as they must have said to Noël Dorgeroux and as they no doubt succeeded in doing with him. It must have been a stirring conversation, from which the great seer derived such power and certainty that it is to him that I will refer, before concluding, in order to add to the discussion the two positive proofs which he himself tried to write at the foot of the screen during the few seconds of his death-struggle, a twofold declaration made by the man, who in departing this life, knew:

"'B-ray.... B E R G E ...'

"When thus expressing his supreme belief in the B-rays, Noël Dorgeroux no longer indicated that unknown radiation which he had once imagined to explain the phenomena of the screen and which would have consisted of the materialization of pictures born within and projected by ourselves. More far-seeing, better-informed as the result of his experiments, abandoning moreover his attempt to connect the new facts with the action of the solar heat which he had so often utilized, he plainly indicated those rays of gravitation of whose existence he had learnt through my pamphlet and also perhaps through his communications with the Venusians, those rays which are habitually employed by them in the same manner as that in which the light-rays are employed by the humblest photographer.

"And the five letters B E R G E are not the first two syllables of the word Bergeronnette. That was the fatal error of which Bérangère Massignac was the victim. They form the word Berger, complete all but the last letter. At the moment of his death, in his already overshadowed brain, Noël Dorgeroux, in order to name Venus, could find no other expression than l'Etoile du Berger, the Shepherd's Star; and his enfeebled hand was able to write only the first few letters. The proof therefore is absolute. The man who knew had time to tell the essential part of what he knew: by means of the rays of gravitation, the Shepherd's Star sends its living messages to the earth.

"If we accept the successive deductions stated in this preliminary essay, which I trust will one day prove to be in a manner a replica of the report stolen from Noël Dorgeroux, there still remain any number of points concerning which we possess not a single element of truth. What is the form of the recording- and projecting-apparatus employed by the Venusians? By what prodigious machinery do they obtain a perfect fixity in the projections between two stars each animated with such complicated movements in space (at present we know of seventeen in the earth alone)? And, to consider only what is close at hand, what is the nature of the screen employed for the Meudon projections? What is that dark-grey substance with which it is coated? How is that substance composed? How is it able to reconstruct the pictures? These are so many questions which our scientific attainments are incapable of solving. But at least we have no right to pronounce them insoluble; and I will go farther and declare that it is our duty to study them by all the means which the public authorities are bound to place at our disposal. This M. Massignac is said to have disappeared from sight. Let the opportunity be seized, let the Meudon Amphitheatre be declared national property! It is out of the question that an individual should, to the detriment of all mankind, remain the sole possessor of such tremendous secrets and have it in his power, if he please and in obedience to a mere whim, to destroy them for all time. The thing cannot be allowed. Before many days have elapsed we must enter into unbroken relations with the inhabitants of Venus. They will tell us the age-old history of our past, reveal to us the great problems which they have elucidated and assist us to benefit by the conquests of a civilization beside which our own as yet seems nothing but confusion, ignorance, the lisping of babes and the stammering of savages...."

CHAPTER XVI

WHERE LIPS UNITE

We have but to read the newspapers of the period, to realize that the excitement caused by the Meudon pictures reached its culminating point as the result of Benjamin Prévotelle's essay. I have four of those newspapers, dated the following day, on my table as I write. Not one of them contains throughout its eight pages a single line that does not refer to what at once became known as the Splendid Theory.

For the rest, the chorus of approval and enthusiasm was general, or very nearly so. There were barely a few cries of vehement protest uttered by experts who felt exasperated by the boldness of the essay even more than by the gaps occurring in it. The great mass of the public saw in all this not a theory but a fact and accepted it as such with the faith of true believers confronted with the divine truth. Every one contributed his own proof as yet one more stone added to the edifice. The objections, however strong they might be—and they were set forth without compromise—seemed temporary and capable of being removed by closer study and a more careful confirmation of the phenomena.

And it is with this conclusion, Benjamin Prévotelle's own conclusion, that all the articles, all the interviews and all the letters that appeared end. The measures recommended by Benjamin Prévotelle were loudly called for. Action must be taken without delay and a series of experiments must be made in the Meudon amphitheatre.

Amid this effervescence, the kidnapping of Massignac went for little. The man Massignac had disappeared? There was nothing to enable one to tell who had carried him off or where he was confined? Very well. It made very little difference. As Benjamin Prévotelle said, the opportunity was too good to miss. The doors of the Yard had been sealed on the first morning. What were we waiting for? Why not begin the experiments at once?

As for me, I did not breathe a word of my Bougival adventure, in the constant fear of implicating Bérangère, who was directly involved in it. All the same, I returned to the banks of the Seine. My rough and ready enquiries showed that Massignac and Velmot had lived on the island during a part of the winter in the company of a small boy who, when they were away, looked after the house which one of them had hired under a false name. I explored the island and the house. No one was living there now. I found a few pieces of furniture, a few household implements, nothing more.

On the fourth day, a provisional committee, appointed ad hoc, met in the Yard about the middle of the afternoon. As the sky was cloudy, they contented themselves with examining the carboys discovered in the basement of the walls and, after lowering the curtain, with cutting off strips of the dark-grey substance at different points of the screen along the edges.

The analysis revealed absolutely nothing out of the way. They found an amalgam of organic materials and acids which it would be tedious to enumerate and which, however employed, supplied not the smallest explanation of the very tiniest phenomena. But, on the sixth day, the sky became clear and the committee returned, together with a number of official persons and mere sightseers who had succeeded in joining them.

The wait in front of the screen was fruitless and just a little ridiculous. All those people looking out for something that did not happen, standing with wide-open eyes and distorted faces, in front of a wall that had nothing on it, wore an air of solemnity which was delightfully comical.

An hour was spent in anxious expectation. The wall remained impassive.

The disappointment was all the greater inasmuch as the public had been waiting for this test as the expected climax of this most sensational tragedy. Were we to give up all hope of knowing the truth and to admit that Noël Dorgeroux's formula alone was capable of producing the pictures? I, for one, was convinced of it. In addition to the substances removed, there was a solution, compounded by Massignac from Noël Dorgeroux's formula, which solution he kept carefully, as my uncle used to do, in blue phials or bottles and which was spread over the screen before each exhibition in order to give it the mysterious power of evoking the images.

A thorough search was instituted, but no phials, no blue bottles came to light.

There was no doubt about it: people were beginning to regret the disappearance, perhaps the death of the man Massignac. Was the great secret to be lost at the very moment when Benjamin Prévotelle's theory had proved its incomparable importance?

Well, on the morning of the eleventh day after the date of Benjamin Prévotelle's essay, that is to say, the 27th of May, the newspapers printed a note signed by Théodore Massignac in which he announced that, in the late afternoon of that same day, the third exhibition in the Yard would take place under his own direction.

He actually appeared at about twelve o'clock in the morning.

The doors were closed and guarded by four detectives and he was unable to obtain admission. But at three o'clock an official from the Prefecture of Police arrived, armed with full powers of negotiation.

Massignac laid down his conditions. He was once more to become the absolute master of the Yard, which was to be surrounded by detectives and closed between the performances to everybody except himself. None of the spectators was to carry a camera or any other instrument.

Everything was conceded; everything was overlooked, in order to continue the interrupted series of miraculous exhibitions and to resume the communications with Venus. This capitulation on the part of the authorities before the audacity of a man whose crime was known to them showed that Benjamin Prévotelle's theory was adopted in government circles.

The fact is—and there was no one who failed to see it—that those in power were giving way in the hope of presently turning the tables and, by some subterfuge, laying hands on the screen at the moment when it was in working-order. Massignac felt this so clearly that, when the doors opened, he had the effrontery to distribute a circular couched in the following terms:

WARNING

"The audience is hereby warned that any attack on the management will have as its immediate consequence the destruction of the screen and the irreparable loss of Noël Dorgeroux's secret."

For my part, as I had had no proof of Massignac's death, I was not surprised at his return. But the alteration in his features and attitude astounded me. He looked ten years older; his figure was bent; and the everlasting smile, which used to be his natural expression, no longer lit up his face, which had become emaciated, yellow and anxious.

He caught sight of me and drew me to one side:

"I say, that scoundrel has played the very devil with me! First he beat me black and blue, down in a cellar. Next he lowered me into the water to make me talk. I was ten days in bed before I got over it! ... By Jingo, it's not his fault if I'm not there now, the villain! ... However, he's had his share too ... and he caught it worse than I did, at least I hope so. The hand that struck him was steady enough and showed no sign of trembling."

I did not ask him what hand he meant or how the tragedy had ended in the darkness. There was only one thing that mattered:

"Massignac, have you read Benjamin Prévotelle's report?"

"Yes."

"Does it agree with the facts? Does it agree with my uncle's account, the one which you've read?"

He shrugged his shoulders:

"What business is that of yours? What business is it of anybody's? Do I keep the pictures to myself? You know I don't. On the contrary, I'm trying to show them to everybody and honestly to earn the money which they pay me. What more do they want?"

"They want to protect a discovery ..."

"Never! Never!" he exclaimed, angrily. "Tell them to shut up and stop all that nonsense! I've bought Noël Dorgeroux's secret, yes, bought and paid for it. Very well, I mean to keep it for myself, for myself alone, against everybody and in spite of any threat. I shan't talk now any more than I did when Velmot had me in his grip and I was on the point of croaking. I tell you, Victorien Beaugrand, Noël Dorgeroux's secret will perish at my death. If I die, it dies: I've taken my oath on it."

When Théodore Massignac, a few minutes later, moved towards his seat, he no longer wore his former air of a lion-tamer entering a cage, but rather the aspect of a hunted animal which is startled by the least sound and trembles at the approach of the man with the whip. But the chuckers-out were there, wearing their ushers' chains and looking as fierce and aggressive as ever. Their wages had been doubled, I was told.

There was no need for the precaution. The danger that threatened Massignac did not come from the crowd, which preserved a religious silence, as though it were preparing to celebrate some solemn ritual. Massignac was received with neither applause nor invective. The spectators waited gravely for what was about to happen, though no one guessed that that was on the point of happening. Those seated on the upper tiers, of whom I was one, often turned their heads upwards. In the clear sky, shimmering with gold, shone Venus, the Evening Star.

What a moment! For the first time in the world's history men felt certain that they were being contemplated by eyes which were not human eyes and watched by minds which differed from their own minds. For the first time they were connected in a tangible fashion with that beyond, formerly peopled by their dreams and their hopes alone, from which the friendly gaze of their new brothers now fell upon them. These were not legends and phantoms projected into the empty heavens by our thirsting souls, but living beings who were addressing us in the living and natural language of

120

the pictures, until the hour, now near at hand, when we should talk together like friends who had lost and found one another.

Their eyes, their Three Eyes, were infinitely gentle that day, filled with a tenderness which seemed born of love and which thrilled us with an equal tenderness, with the same love. What were they presaging, those women's eyes, those eyes of many women that quivered before us so attractively and with such smiles and such delightful promise? Of what happy and charming scenes of our past were we to be the astonished witnesses?

I watched my neighbours. All, like myself, were leaning towards the screen. The sight affected their faces before it occurred. I noticed the pallor of two young men beside me. A woman whose face was hidden from my eyes by a thick mourning-veil sat with her handkerchief in her hand, ready to shed tears.

The first scene represented a landscape, full of glaring light, which appeared to be an Italian landscape, with a dusty road along which cavalry-men, wearing the uniform of the revolutionary armies, were galloping around a travelling-carriage drawn by four horses. Then, immediately afterwards, we saw in a shady garden, at the end of an avenue of dark cypresses, a house with closed shutters standing on a flower-decked terrace.

The carriage stopped at the foot of the terrace and drove off again after setting down an officer who ran up to the door and knocked at it with the pommel of his sword.

The door was opened almost at once. A tall young woman rushed out of the house, with her arms outstretched towards the officer. But, at the moment when they were about to embrace, they both took a few steps backwards, as though to delay their happiness and in so doing to taste its delights more fully.

Then the screen showed us the woman's face; and words cannot depict the expression of joy and headlong love that turned this face, which was neither very beautiful nor very young, into something more alive with youth and beauty than anything in this world.

After that, the lovers flung themselves into each others' arms, as though their lives, too long separated, were striving to make but one. Their lips united.

We saw nothing more of the French officer and his Italian lover. A new picture followed, less bright but equally clear, the picture of a long, battlemented rampart, marked with a series of round, machicolated towers. Below and in the centre, among the ruins of a bastion, were trees growing in a semicircle around an ancient oak-tree.

Gradually, from the shade of the trees, there stepped into the sunlight a quite young girl, clad in the pointed head-dress of the

121

fifteenth century and a full-skirted gown trailing along the ground. She stopped with her hands open and raised on high. She saw something that we were unable to see. She wore a bewitching smile. Her eyes were half-closed; and her slender figure seemed to sway as she waited.

What she was awaiting was the arrival of a young page, who came to her and kissed her lips while she flung herself on his shoulder.

This enamoured couple certainly moved us, as the first couple had done, by reason of the passion and the languor that possessed them, but even more by reason of the thought that they were an actual couple, living, before our eyes and at the present day, their real life of long ago. Our sensations were no longer such as we experienced at the earlier exhibitions. They had then been full of hesitation and ignorance. We now knew. In this late period of the world's existence, we were beholding the life of human beings of the fifteenth century. They were not repeating for our entertainment actions which had been performed before. They were performing them for the first occasion in time and space. It was their first kiss of love.

This, the feeling that one is seeing this, is a feeling which surpasses everything that can be imagined! To see a fifteenth-century page and damsel kissing each other on the lips!

To see, as we saw immediately afterwards, a Greek hill! To see the Acropolis standing against its sky of two thousand years ago, with its houses and gardens, its palm-trees, its lanes, its vestibules and temples, the Parthenon, not in ruins, but in all its splendour and perfection! A host of statues surround it. Men and women climb its stairways. And these men and women are Athenians of the time of Pericles or Demosthenes!

They come and go in all directions. They talk together. Then they drift away. A little empty street runs down between two white walls. A group passes and moves away, leaving behind it a man and woman who stop suddenly, glance around them and kiss each other fervently. And we see, underneath the veil in which the woman's forehead is shrouded, two great, black eyes whose lids flutter like wings, eyes which open, close, laugh and weep.

Thus we go back through the ages and we understand that those who, gazing down upon the earth, have taken these successive pictures wish, in displaying them to us, to show us the act, for-ever youthful and eternally renewed, of that universal love of which they proclaim themselves, like us, to be the slaves and the zealous worshippers. They too are governed and exalted by the same law, though perhaps not expressed in them by the intoxication of a like caress. The same impulse sweeps them along. But do they know the adorable union of the lips?

Other couples passed. Other periods were reviewed. Other civilizations appeared to us. We saw the kiss of an Egyptian peasant and a young girl; and that exchanged high up in a hanging garden of Babylon between a princess and a priest; and that which transfigured to such a degree as to make them almost human two unspeakable beings squatting at the door of a prehistoric cave; and more kisses and yet more.

They were brief visions, some of which were indistinct and faded, like the colours of an ancient fresco, but yet searching and potent, because of the meaning which they assumed, full at the same time of poetry and brutal reality, of violence and serene loveliness.

And always the woman's eyes were the centre, the purpose, as it were the justification of the pictures. Oh, the smiles and the tears, the gladness and the despair and the exquisite rapture of all those eyes! How our friends up aloft must also have felt all the charm of them, thus to dedicate them to us! How they must have felt and perhaps regretted all the difference between those eyes of ecstasy and enchantment and their own eyes, so gloomy and void of all expression! There was such sweetness in those women's eyes, such grace, such ingenuousness, such adorable perfidy, such distress and such seductiveness, such triumphant joy, such grateful humility ... and such love, when they offered their submissive lips to the man!

I was unable to see the end of those pictures. There was a movement round about me in the midst of the crowd, which was beside itself with painful excitement; and I found myself next to a woman in mourning, whose face was hidden beneath her veils.

She thrust these aside. I recognized Bérangère. She raised her passionate eyes to mine, flung her arms round my neck and gave me her lips, while she stammered words of love. And in this way I learnt, without any need of explanation, that Massignac's insinuations against his daughter were false, that she was the terror-stricken victim of the two scoundrels and that she had never ceased to love me.

CHAPTER XVII

SUPREME VISIONS

The exhibition of the following day was preceded by two important pieces of news which appeared in the evening papers. A group of financiers had offered Théodore Massignac the sum of ten million francs in consideration of Noël Dorgeroux's secret and the right to work the amphitheatre. Théodore Massignac was to give them his answer next day.

But, at the last moment, a telegram from the south of France announced that the maid-of-all-work who had nursed Massignac in his house at Toulouse, a few weeks before, now declared that her master's illness was feigned and that Massignac had left the house on several occasions, each time carefully concealing his absence from all the neighbours. Now one of these absences synchronized with the murder of Noël Dorgeroux. The woman's accusation therefore obliged the authorities to reopen an enquiry which had already elicited so much presumptive evidence of Théodore Massignac's guilt.

The upshot of these two pieces of news was that my uncle Dorgeroux's secret depended on chance, that it would be saved by an immediate purchase or lost for ever by Massignac's arrest. This alternative added still further to the anxious curiosity of the spectators, many of whom correctly believed that they were witnessing the last of the Meudon exhibitions. They discussed the articles in the papers and the proofs or objections accumulated for or against the theory. They said that Prévotelle, to whom Massignac was refusing admission to the amphitheatre, was preparing a whole series of experiments with the intention of proving the absolute accuracy of his theory, the simplest of which experiments consisted in erecting a scaffolding outside the Yard and setting up an intervening obstacle to intercept the rays that passed from Venus to the screen.

I myself who, since the previous day, had thought of nothing but Bérangère, whom I had pursued in vain through the crowd amid which she had succeeded in escaping me, I myself was smitten with the fever and that day abandoned the attempt to discover upon the close-packed tiers of seats the mysterious girl whom I had held to me all quivering, happy to abandon herself for a few moments to a kiss on which she bestowed all the fervour of her incomprehensible soul. I forgot her. The screen alone counted, to my mind. The problem of my life was swallowed up in the great riddle which those solemn minutes in the history of mankind set before us.

They began, after the most sorrowful and heart-rending look that had yet animated the miraculous Three Eyes, they began with that singular phantasmagoria of creatures which Benjamin Prévotelle proposed that we should regard as the inhabitants of Venus and which, for that matter, it was impossible that we should not so regard. I will not try to define them with greater precision nor to describe the setting in which they moved. One's confusion in the presence of those grotesque Shapes, those absurd movements and those startling landscapes was so great that one had hardly time to receive very exact impressions or to deduce the slightest theory from them. All that I can say is that we were the observers, as on the first occasion, of a manifestation of public order. There were numbers of spectators and a connected sequence of actions tending towards a clearly-defined end, which seemed to us to be of the same nature as the first execution. Everything, in fact—the grouping of certain Shapes in the middle of an empty space and around a motionless Shape, the actions performed, the cutting up of that isolated Shape—suggested that there was an execution in progress, the taking of a life. In any case, we were perfectly well aware, through the corresponding instance, that its real significance resided only in the second part of the film. Since nearly all the pictures were twofold, impressing us by antithesis or analogy, we must wait awhile to catch the general idea which directed this projection.

This soon became apparent; and the mere narrative of what we saw showed how right my uncle Dorgeroux's prophecy was when he said:

"Men will come here as pilgrims and will fall upon their knees and weep like children!"

A winding road, rough with cobbles and cut into steps, climbs a steep, arid, shadowless hill under a burning sun. We almost seem to see the eddies rising, like a scorching breath, from the parched soil.

A mob of excited people is scaling the abrupt slope. On their backs hang tattered robes; their aspect is that of the beggars or artisans of an eastern populace.

The road disappears and appears again at a higher level, where we see that this mob is preceding and following a company consisting of soldiers clad like the Roman legionaires. There are sixty or eighty of them, perhaps. They are marching slowly, in a ragged body, carrying their spears over their shoulders, while some are swinging their helmets in their hands. Now and again one stops to drink.

125

From time to time we become aware that these soldiers are serving as escort to a central group, consisting of a few officers and of civilians clad in long robes, like priests, and, a little apart from them, four women, the lower half of whose faces is hidden by a long veil. Then, suddenly at a turn in the road, where the group has become slightly disorganized, we see a heavy cross outspread, jolting its way upwards. A man is underneath, as it were crushed by the intolerable burden which he is condemned to bear to the place of martyrdom. He stumbles at each step, makes an effort, stands up again, falls again, drags himself yet a little farther, crawling, clutching at the stones on the road, and then moves no more. A blow from a staff, administered by one of the soldiers, makes no difference. His strength is exhausted.

At that moment, a man comes down the stony path. He is stopped and ordered to carry the cross. He cannot and quickly makes his escape. But, as the soldiers with their spears turn back towards the man lying on the ground, behold, three of the women intervene and offer to carry the burden. One of them takes the end, the two others take the two arms and thus they climb the rugged hill, while the fourth woman raises the condemned man and supports his hesitating steps.

At two further points we are able to follow the painful ascent of him who is going to his death. And on each occasion his face is shown by itself upon the screen. We do not recognize it. It is unlike the face which we expected to see, according to the usual representations. But how much more fully satisfied the profound conception which it evokes in us by its actual presence!

It is He: we cannot for a moment doubt it. He lives before us. He is suffering. He is about to die before us. He is about to die. Each of us would fain avert the menace of that horrible death; and each of us prays with all his might for some peaceful vision in which we may see Him surrounded by His Disciples and His gentle womenfolk. The soldiers, as they reach the place of torture, assume a harsher aspect. The priests with ritual gestures curse the stones amid which the tree is to be raised and retire, with hanging heads.

Here comes the cross, with the women bending under it. The condemned man follows them. There are two of them now supporting Him. He stops. Nothing can save Him now. When we see Him again, after a short interruption of the picture, the cross is set up and the agony has begun.

I do not believe that any assembly of men was ever thrilled by a more violent and noble emotion than that which held us in its grip at this hour, which, let it be clearly understood, was the very hour at which the world's destiny was settled for centuries and centuries.

We were not guessing at it through legends and distorted narratives. We did not have to reconstruct it after uncertain documents or to conceive it according to our own feelings and imagination. It was there, that unparalleled hour. It lived before us, in a setting devoid of grandeur, a setting which seemed to us very lowly, very poverty-stricken. The bulk of the sightseers had departed. A dozen soldiers were dicing on a flat stone and drinking. Four women were standing in the shadow of a man crucified whose feet they bathed with their tears. At the summit of two other hillocks hard by, two figures were writhing on their crosses. That was all.

But what a meaning we read into this gloomy spectacle! What a frightful tragedy was enacted before our eyes! The beating of our hearts wrung with love and distress was the very beating of that Sacred Heart. Those weary eyes looked down upon the same things that we beheld, the same dry soil, the same savage faces of the soldiers, the same countenances of the grief-stricken women.

When a last vision showed us His rigid and emaciated body and His sweet ravaged head in which the dilated eyes seemed to us abnormally large, the whole crowd rose to its feet, men and women fell upon their knees and, in a profound silence that quivered with prayer, all arms were despairingly outstretched towards the dying God.

Such scenes cannot be understood by those who did not witness them. You will no more find their living presentment in the pages in which I describe them than I can find it in the newspapers of the time. The latter pile up adjectives, exclamations and apostrophes which give no idea of what the vivid reality was. On the other hand, all the articles lay stress upon the essential truth which emerges from the two films of that day and, very rightly, declare that the second explains and completes the first. Yonder also, among our distant brethren, a God was delivered to the horrors of martyrdom; and, by connecting the two events, they intended to convey to us that, like ourselves, they possessed a religious belief and ideal aspirations. In the same way, they had shown us by the death of one of their rulers and the death of one of our kings that they had known the same political upheavals. In the same way, they had shown us by visions of lovers that, like us, they yielded to the power of love. Therefore, the same stages of civilizations, the same efforts of belief, the same instincts, the same sentiments existed in both worlds.

How could messages so positive, so stimulating have failed to increase our longing to know more about it all and to communicate more closely? How could we do other than think of the questions which it was possible to put and of the problems which would be elucidated, problems of the future and the past, problems of civilization, problems of destiny?

But the same uncertainty lingered in us, keener than the day before. What would become of Noël Dorgeroux's secret? The position was this: Massignac accepted the ten millions which he was offered, but on condition that he was paid the money immediately after the performance and that he received a safe-conduct for America. Now, although the enquiries instituted at Toulouse confirmed the accusations brought against him by the maid-of-all-work, it was stated that the compact was on the point of being concluded, so greatly did the importance of Noël Dorgeroux's secret outweigh all ordinary consideration of justice and punishment. Finding itself confronted with a state of things which could not be prolonged, the government was yielding, though constraining Massignac to sell the secret under penalty of immediate arrest and posting all around him men who were instructed to lay him by the heels at the first sign of any trickery. When the iron curtain fell, twelve policemen took the place of the usual attendants.

And then began an exhibition to which special circumstances imparted so great a gravity and which was in itself so poignant and so implacable.

As on the other occasions, we did not at first grasp the significance which the scenes projected on the screen were intended to convey. These scenes passed before our eyes as swiftly as the love-scenes displayed two days before.

There was not the initial vision of the Three Eyes. We plunged straight into reality. In the middle of a garden sat a woman, young still and beautiful, dressed in the fashion of 1830. She was working at a tapestry stretched on a frame and from time to time raised her eyes to cast a fond look at a little girl playing by her side. The mother and child smiled at each other. The child left her sand-pies and came and kissed her mother.

For a few minutes there was merely this placid picture of human life.

Then, a dozen paces behind the mother, a tall, close-trimmed screen of foliage is gently thrust aside and, with a series of imperceptible movements, a man comes out of the shadow, a man, like the woman, young and well-dressed.

His face is hard, his jaws are set. He has a knife in his hand.

He takes three or four steps forward. The woman does not hear him, the little girl cannot see him. He comes still farther forward, with infinite precautions, so that the gravel may not creak under his feet nor any branch touch him.

128

He stands over the woman. His face displays a terrible cruelty and an inflexible will. The woman's face is still smiling and happy.

Slowly his arm is raised above that smile, above that happiness. Then it descends, with equal slowness; and suddenly, beneath the left shoulder, it strikes a sharp blow at the heart.

There is not a sound; that is certain. At most, a sigh, like the one sigh emitted, in the awful silence, by the crowd in the Yard.

The man has withdrawn his weapon. He listens for a moment, bends over the lifeless body that has huddled into the chair, feels the hand and then steals back with measured steps to the screen of foliage, which closes behind him.

The child has not ceased playing. She continues to laugh and talk.

The picture fades away.

The next shows us two men walking along a deserted path, beside which flows a narrow river. They are talking without animation; they might be discussing the weather.

When they turn round and retrace their steps, we see that one of the two men, the one who hitherto had been hidden behind his companion, carries a revolver.

They both stop and continue to talk quietly. But the face of the armed man becomes distorted and assumes the same criminal expression which we beheld in the first murderer. And suddenly he makes a movement of attack and fires; the other falls; and the first flings himself upon him and snatches a pocket-book from him.

There were four more murders, none of which had as its perpetrator or its victim any one who was known to us. They were so many sensational incidents, very short, restricted to the essential factors; the peaceful representation of a scene in daily life and the sudden explosion of crime in all its bestial horror.

The sight was dreadful, especially because of the expression of confidence and serenity maintained by the victim, while we, in the audience, saw the phantom of death rise over him. The waiting for the blow which we were unable to avert left us breathless and terrified.

And one last picture of a man appeared to us. A stifled exclamation rose from the crowd. It was Noël Dorgeroux.

CHAPTER XVIII

THE CHÂTEAU DE PRÉ-BONY

The exclamation of the crowd proved to me that, at the sight of the great old man, who was known to all by his portraits and by the posters exhibited at the doors of the Yard, the same thought had instantaneously struck us all. We understood from the first. After the series of criminal pictures, we knew the meaning of Noël Dorgeroux's appearance on the screen and knew the inexorable climax of the story which we were being told. There had been six victims. My uncle would be the seventh. We were going to witness his death and to see the face of the murderer.

All this was planned with the most disconcerting skill and with a logic whose implacable rigour wrung our very souls. We were as though imprisoned in a horribly painful track which we were bound to follow to the end, notwithstanding the unspeakable violence of our sensations. I sometimes ask myself, in all sincerity, whether the series of miraculous visions could have been continued much longer, so far did the nervous tension which they demanded exceed our human strength.

A succession of pictures showed us several episodes of which the first dated back to a period when Noël Dorgeroux certainly had not discovered the great secret, for his son was still alive. It was the time of the war. Dominique, in uniform, was embracing the old fellow, who was weeping and trying to hold him back; and, when Dominique went, Noël Dorgeroux watched him go with all the distress of a father who is not to see his son again.

Next we have him again, once more in the Yard, which is encumbered with its sheds and workshops, as it used to be. Bérangère, quite a child, is running to and fro. She is thirteen or fourteen at most.

We now follow their existence in pictures which tell us with what hourly attention my uncle Dorgeroux's labours were watched from up yonder. He became old and bent. The little one grew up, which did not deter her from playing and running about.

On the day when we are to see her as I had found her in the previous summer, we see at the same time Noël Dorgeroux standing on a ladder and daubing the wall with a long brush which he keeps dipping into a can. He steps back and looks with a questioning gaze at the wall where the screen is marked out. There is nothing. Nevertheless something vague and confused must already have throbbed in the heart of the substance, because he seems to be waiting and seeking. . . .

A click; and everything is changed. The amphitheatre arises, unfinished in parts, as it was on the Sunday in March when I discovered my uncle's dead body. The new wall is there, surrounded by its canopy. My uncle has opened the recess contained in the basement and is arranging his carboys.

But, now, beyond the amphitheatre, which grows smaller for an instant, we see the trees in the woods and the undulations of the adjoining meadow; and a man comes up on that side and moves towards the path which skirts the fence. I for my part recognize his figure. It is the man with whom I was to struggle, half an hour later, in the wood through which he had just come. It is the murderer. He is wrapped in a rain-coat whose upturned collar touches the lowered brim of his hat. He walks uneasily. He goes up to the lamp-post, looks around him, climbs up slowly and makes his way into the Yard. He follows the road which I myself took that day after him and thrusts forward his head as I did.

Noël Dorgeroux is standing before the screen. He has closed the recess and jotted down some notes in a book. The victim suspects nothing.

Then the man throws off his wrap and his hat. He turns his face in our direction. It is Massignac.

The crowd was so much expecting to find that it was he that there was no demonstration of surprise. Besides, the pictures on this day were of a nature that left no room for alien thoughts or impressions. The consequences which might ensue from the public proof of Massignac's guilt were not apparent to us. We were not living through the minutes which were elapsing in the past but through those which were elapsing in the present; and until the last moment we thought only of knowing whether Noël Dorgeroux, whom we knew to be dead, was going to be murdered.

The scene did not last long. In reality my uncle was not conscious for a second of the danger that threatened him; and, contrary to what was elicited at the enquiry, there was no trace of that struggle of which the signs appeared to have been discovered. This struggle occurred afterwards, when my uncle had been struck down and was lying on the ground, motionless. It took place between a murderer seized with insensate fury and the corpse which he seemed bent upon killing anew.

And in fact it was this act of savage brutality that let loose the rage of the crowd. Held back until then by a sort of unreasoning hope and petrified, in its terror, at the sight of the loathsome act accomplished on the screen, it was stirred with anger and hatred against the living and visible murderer whose existence suddenly provoked it beyond endurance. It experienced a sense of revolt and a need for immediate justice which no considerations were able to stay. It underwent an immediate change of attitude. It withdrew itself abruptly from any sort of memory or evocation of the past, to fling itself into the reality of the present and to play its part in the necessary action. And, obeying an unanimous impulse, pouring helter-skelter down the tiers and flowing like a torrent through every gangway, it rushed to the assault of the iron cage in which Massignac was sheltering.

I cannot describe exactly the manner in which things took place. Massignac, who attempted to take flight at the first moment of the accusation, found in front of him the twelve policemen, who next turned against the crowd when it came dashing against the rails of the high grille. But what resistance were those twelve men able to offer? The grille fell. The police were borne down in the crush. In a flash I saw Massignac braced against the wall and taking aim with two revolvers held in his outstretched hands. A number of shots rang out. Some of the aggressors dropped. Then Massignac, taking advantage of the hesitation which kept back the others, stooped swiftly towards the electric battery in the foundation. He pressed a button. Right at the top of the wall, the canopy overhanging the two pillars opened like a sluice and sent forth streams of a bluish liquid, which seethed and bubbled in a cascade over the whole surface of the screen.

I then remembered Massignac's terrible prophecy:

"If I die, it means the death of Noël Dorgeroux's secret. We shall perish together."

In the anguish of peril, at the very bottom of the abyss, he had conceived the abominable idea and had the courage to carry out his threat. My uncle's work was utterly destroyed.

Nevertheless I darted forward, as though I could still avert the disaster by saving the scoundrel's life. But the crowd had seized upon its prey and was passing it from hand to hand, like a howling pack worrying and rending the animal which it had hunted down.

I succeeded in shouldering my way through with the aid of two policemen and then only because Massignac's body had ended by falling into the hands of a band of less infuriated assailants, who were embarrassed by the sight of the dying man. They formed themselves into a group to protect his death-struggles and one of them even, raising his voice above the din, called to me:

"Quick, quick!" he said, when I came near. "He is speaking your name."

At the first glance at the mass of bleeding flesh that lay on one of the tiers, between two rows of seats, I perceived that there was no hope and that it was a miracle that this corpse was still breathing. Still it was uttering my name. I caught the syllables as I stooped over the face mauled beyond recognition and, speaking slowly and distinctly, I said:

"It's I, Massignac, it's Victorien Beaugrand. What have you to say to me?"

He managed to lift his eyelids, looked at me with a dim eye which closed again immediately and stammered:

"A letter ... a letter ... sewn in the lining...."

I felt the rags of cloth which remained of his jacket. Massignac had done well to sew up the letter, for all the other papers had left his pocket. I at once read my name on the envelope.

"Open it ... open it," he said, in a whisper.

I tore open the envelope. There were only a few lines scribbled in a large hand across the sheet of paper, a few lines of which I took the time to read only the first, which said:

"Bérangère knows the formula."

"Bérangère!" I exclaimed. "But where is she? Do you know?"

I at once understood the imprudence of which I had been guilty in thus mentioning the girl's name aloud; and, bending lower down, I put my ear to Massignac's mouth to catch his last words.

He repeated the name of Bérangère time after time, in the effort to pronounce the answer which I asked for and which his memory perhaps refused to supply. His lips moved convulsively and he stammered forth some hoarse sounds which were more like a death-rattle but which yet enabled me to distinguish the words:

"Bérangère.... Château ... Château de Pré-Bony...."

However great the tension of the mind may be when concentrated on an idea which entirely absorbs it, we remain more or less subject to the thousand sensations that assail us. Thus, at the very moment when I rose and, in a whisper, repeated, "Château de Pré-Bony ... de Pré-Bony," the vague impression that another had heard the address which Massignac had given began to take shape and consistency within me. Nay more, I perceived, when it was too late, that this other man, thanks to his position at my side, must have been able to read as I had read, the opening words of Théodore Massignac's letter. And that other man's able make-up suddenly dropped away before my eyes to reveal the pallid features of the man Velmot.

I turned my head. The man had just made his way out of the band of onlookers who stood gathered round us and was slipping through the shifting masses of the crowd. I called out. I shouted his name. I dragged detectives in his wake. It was too late.

And so the man Velmot, the implacable enemy who had not hesitated to torture Massignac in order to extract my uncle Dorgeroux's formula from him, knew that Bérangère was acquainted with the formula! And he had at the same time learnt, what he doubtless did not know before, where Bérangère was concealed.

The Château de Pré-Bony! Where was this country-house? In what corner of France had Bérangère taken refuge after the murder of her god-father? It could not be very far from Paris, seeing that she had once asked for my assistance and that, two days ago, she had come to the Yard. But, whatever the distance, how was I to find it? There were a thousand country-houses within a radius of twenty-five miles from Paris.

"And yet," I said to myself, "the solution of the tragedy lies there, in that country-house. All is not lost and all may still be saved, but I have to get there. Though, the miraculous screen is destroyed, Massignac has given me the means of reconstructing it, but I have to get there. And I have to get there by day break, or Velmot will have Bérangère at his mercy."

I spent the whole evening in enquiries. I consulted maps, gazetteers, directories. I asked everywhere; I telephoned. No one was able to supply the least hint as to the whereabouts of the Château de Pré-Bony.

It was not until the morning, after an agitated night, that a more methodical scrutiny of recent events gave me the idea of beginning my investigations in the actual district where I knew that Bérangère had stayed. I hired a motor-car and had myself driven towards Bougival. I had no great hope. But my fear lest Velmot should discover Bérangère's retreat before I did caused me such intense suffering that I never ceased repeating to myself:

"That's it.... I'm on the right track.... I'm certain to find Bérangère; and the villain shall not touch a hair of her head."

My love for the girl suddenly became purged of all the doubts and suspicions that had poisoned it. For the rest, I did not trouble about these details and troubled myself neither to explain her conduct nor to establish the least proof for or against her. Even if her kiss had not already wiped out every disagreeable recollection, the danger which she was incurring was enough to restore all my faith in her and all my affection.

My first enquiries at Ville d'Avray, Marnes and Vaucresson told me nothing. The Château de Pré-Bony was unknown. At La Cello-Saint-Cloud I encountered a fresh check. But here, in an inn, I seemed to recover, thanks to the accident of a casual question, the traces of the man Velmot: a tall, white-faced gentleman, I was told, who often motored along the Bougival road and who had been seen prowling outside the village that very morning.

I questioned my informant more closely. It really was Velmot. He had four hours' start of me. And he knew where to go! And he was in love with Bérangère! Four hours' start, for that clever and daring scoundrel, who was staking his all on this last throw of the die! Who could stop him? What scruples had he? To seize upon Bérangère, to hold her in his power, to compel her to speak: all this was now mere child's play. And he was in love with Bérangère!

I remember striking the inn-table with my fist and exclaiming, angrily:

"No, no, it's not possible! ... The house in question is bound to be somewhere near here! ... They must show me the way!"

Thenceforward I did not experience a moment's hesitation. On the one hand, I was not mistaken in coming to this district. On the other hand, I knew that Velmot, having heard what Massignac said and knowing the country by having lived in it, had begun his campaign at dawn.

There was a crowd of people outside the inn. Feverishly I put the questions which remained unanswered. At last, some one mentioned a cross-roads which was sometimes known by the name of Pré-Bony and which was on the Saint-Cucufa road, some two or three miles away. One of the roads which branched from it led to a new house, of not very imposing appearance, which was inhabited by a young married couple, the Comte and Comtesse de Roncherolles.

I really had the impression that it was my sheer will-power that had brought about this favourable incident and, so to speak, created, lock, stock and barrel and within my reach, that unknown country-house which it behoved me to visit that very instant.

I made my way there hurriedly. At the moment when I was walking across the garden, a young man alighted from horseback at the foot of the steps.

"Is this the Château de Pré-Bony?" I asked.

He flung the reins of his horse to a groom and replied, with a smile:

"At least that is what they call it, a little pompously, at Bougival."

"Oh," I murmured, as though taken aback by an unhoped for piece of news, "it's here ... and I am in time!"

The young man introduced himself. It was the Comte de Roncherolles.

"May I ask to whom I have the honour ..."

"Victorien Beaugrand," I replied.

And, without further preamble, confiding in the man's looks, which were frank and friendly, I said:

"I have come about Bérangère. She's here, isn't she? She has found a shelter here?"

The Comte de Roncherolles flushed slightly and eyed me with a certain attention. I took his hand:

"If you please, monsieur, the position is very serious. Bérangère is being hunted down by an extremely dangerous man."

"Who is that?"

"Velmot."

"Velmot?"

The count threw off all further disguise as useless and repeated:

"Velmot! Velmot! The enemy whom she loathes! ... Yes, she has everything to fear from the man. Fortunately, he does not know where she is."

"He does know ... since yesterday," I exclaimed.

"Granted. But he will need time to make his preparations, to plan his move."

"He was seen not far from here, yesterday, by people of the village."

I began to tell him what I knew. He did not wait for me to finish. Evidently as anxious as myself, he drew me towards a lodge, standing some distance from the house, which Bérangère occupied.

He knocked. There was no answer. But the door was open. He entered and went upstairs to Bérangère's room. She was not there.

He did not seem greatly surprised.

"She often goes out early," he said.

"Perhaps she is at the house?" I suggested.

"With my wife? No, my wife is not very well and would not be up yet."

"What then?"

"I presume she has gone for her ordinary walk to the ruins of the old castle. She likes the view there, which embraces Bougival and the whole river."

"Is it far?"

"No, just at the end of the park."

Nevertheless the park stretched some way back; and it took us four or five minutes' walk to reach a circular clearing from which we could see a few lengths of broken wall perched on the top of a ridge among some fallen heaps of stone-work.

"There," said the count. "Bérangère has been to this bench. She has left the book which she was reading."

"And a scarf too," I said, anxiously. "Look, a rumpled scarf....

And the grass round about shows signs of having been trampled on…. My God, I hope nothing has happened to the poor child!"

I had not finished speaking when we heard cries from the direction of the ruins, cries for help or cries of pain, we could not tell which. We at once darted along the narrow path which ran up the hill, cutting across the winding forest-road. When we were half-way up, the cries broke out again; and a woman's figure came into view among the crumbling stones of the old castle.

"Bérangère!" I cried, increasing my pace.

She did not see me. She was running, as though she had some one in pursuit of her, and taking advantage of every bit of shelter that the ruins offered. Presently a man appeared, looking for her and threatening her with a revolver which he carried in his hand.

"It's he!" I stammered. "It's Velmot!"

One after the other they entered the huddle of ruins, from which we were now separated by forty yards at most. We covered the distance in a few seconds and I rushed ahead towards the place through which Bérangère had slipped.

As I arrived, a shot rang out, some little way off, and I heard moans. Despite my efforts, I could get no farther forward, because the passage was blocked by brambles and trails of ivy. My companion and I struggled desperately against the branches which were cutting our faces. At length we emerged on a large platform, where at first we saw no one among the tall grass and the moss-grown rocks. Still, there was that shot … and those cries of pain quite close to where we stood. . . .

Suddenly the count, who was searching a short distance in front of me, exclaimed:

"There she is! … Bérangère! Are you hurt?"

I leapt towards him. Bérangère lay outstretched in a tangle of leaves and herbage.

She was so pale that I had not a doubt but that she was dead; and I felt very clearly that I should not be able to survive her. I even completed my thought by saying, aloud:

"I will avenge her first. The murderer shall die by my hand, I swear it."

But the count, after a hurried inspection, declared.

"She's not dead, she's breathing."

And I saw her open her eyes.

I fell on my knees besides her and, lifting her fair and sorrow-stricken face in my hands, asked her:

"Where are you hurt, Bérangère? Tell me, darling."

"I'm not hurt," she whispered. "It's the exertion, the excitement."

"But surely," I insisted, "he fired at you?"

"No, no," she said, "it was I who fired."

"Do you mean that? You fired?"

"Yes, with his revolver."

"But you missed him. He has made his escape."

"I did not miss him. I saw him fall ... quite close to this ... on the edge of the ravine."

This ravine was a deep cut in the ground, on our right. The count went to the spot and called to me. When I was standing beside him, he showed me the body of a man lying head downwards, his face covered with blood. I approached and recognized Velmot. He was dead.

CHAPTER XIX

THE FORMULA

Velmot dead, Bérangère alive: the joy of it! The sudden sense of security! This time, the evil adventure was over, since the girl whom I loved had nothing more to fear. And my thoughts at once harked back to Noël Dorgeroux: the formula in which the great secret was summed up was saved. With the clues and the means of action which existed elsewhere, mankind was now in a position to continue my uncle's work.

Bérangère called me back:

"He's dead, isn't he?"

I felt intuitively that I ought not to tell her a truth which was too heavy for her to bear and which she was afraid of hearing and I declared:

"Not at all.... We haven't seen him.... He must have got away...."

My answer seemed to relieve her; and she whispered:

"In any case, he is wounded.... I know I hit him."

"Rest, my darling," I said, "and don't worry any more about anything."

She did as she was told; and she was so weary that she soon fell asleep.

Before taking her home, the count and I went back to the body and lowered it down the slope of the ravine, which we followed to the wall that surrounded the estate. As there was a breach at this spot, the count gave it as his opinion that Velmot could not have entered anywhere but here. And in fact a little lower down, at the entrance to a lonely forest-road we discovered his car. We lifted the body into it, placed the revolver on the seat, drove the car to a distance of half a mile and left it at the entrance to a clearing. We met nobody on the road. The death would beyond a doubt be ascribed to suicide.

An hour later, Bérangère, now back to the lodge and lying on her bed, gave me her hand, which I covered with kisses. We were alone, with no more enemies around us. There was no hideous shape prowling in the dark. No one was any longer able to thwart our rightful happiness.

"The nightmare has passed," I said. "There is no obstacle left between you and me. You will no longer try to run away, will you?"

I watched her with an emotion in which still lingered no small anxiety. Dear little girl, she was still, to me, a creature full of mystery and the unknown; and there were many secrets hidden in the shadowy places of that soul into which I had never entered. I told her as much. She in her turn looked at me for a long time, with her tired and fevered eyes, so different from the careless, laughing eyes which I had loved long ago, and she whispered:

"Secrets? My secrets? No. There is only one secret in me; and that one secret is the cause of everything."

"May I hear it?"

"I love you."

I felt a thrill of joy. Often I had experienced a profound intuition of this love of hers, but it had been spoilt by so much distrust, suspicion and resentment. And now Bérangère was confessing it to me, gravely and frankly.

"You love me," I repeated. "You love me. Why did you not tell me earlier? How many misfortunes would have been avoided! Why didn't you?"

"I couldn't."

"And you can now, because there is no longer any obstacle between us?"

"There is the same obstacle as ever."

"Which is that?"

"My father."

I said in a lower voice:

"Yon know that Théodore Massignac is dead?"

"Yes."

"Well, then?"

"I am Théodore Massignac's daughter."

I cried eagerly:

"Bérangère, there is something I want to tell you; and I assure you beforehand ..."

She interrupted me:

"Please don't say anything more. There's always that between us. It is a gulf which we cannot hope to fill with words."

She seemed so much exhausted that I made a movement to leave her. She stopped me:

"No," she said, "don't go. I am not going to be ill ... for more than a day or two, at the outside. First of all, I want everything to be quite clear between us; I want you to understand every single thing that I have done. Listen to me...."

"To-morrow, Bérangère."

"No, to-day," she insisted. "I feel a need to tell you at once what I have to say. Nothing will do more to restore my peace of mind. Listen to me...."

She did not have to entreat me long. How could I have wearied of looking at her and listening to her? We had been through such trials when separated from each other that I was afraid, after all, of being parted from her now.

She put her arm round my neck. Her beautiful lips were quivering beneath my eyes. Seeing my gaze fixed upon them, she smiled:

"You remember, in the Yard ... the first time.... From that day, I hated you ... and adored you.... I was your enemy ... and your slave.... Yes, all my independent and rather wild nature was up in arms at not being able to shake off a recollection which gave me so much pain ... and so much pleasure! ... I was mastered. I ran away from you. I kept on coming back to you ... and I should have come back altogether, if that man—you know whom I mean—had not spoken to me one morning...."

"Velmot! What did he come for? What did he want?"

"He came from my father. What he wanted, as I perceived later, was through me to enter into Noël Dorgeroux's life and rob him of the secret of his invention."

"Why did you not warn me?"

"From the first moment, Velmot asked me to be silent. Later, he commanded it."

"You ought not to have obeyed him...."

"Had I committed the least indiscretion, he would have killed you. I loved you. I was afraid; and I was all the more afraid because Velmot persecuted me with a love which my hatred for him merely stimulated. How could I doubt that his threat was seriously meant? From that time onward, I was caught in the wheels of the machine. What with one lie and another, I became his accomplice ... or rather their accomplice, for my father joined him in the course of the winter. Oh, the torture of it! That man who loved me ... and that contemptible father! ... I lived a life of horror ... always hoping that they would grow tired because their machinations were leading to nothing."

"And what about my letters from Grenoble? And my uncle's fears?"

"Yes, I know, my uncle often mentioned them to me; and, without revealing the plot to him, I myself put him on his guard. It was at my request that he sent you that report which was stolen. Only, he never anticipated murder. Theft, yes; and, notwithstanding the watch which I maintained, I could see that I was doing no good, that my father made his way into the Lodge at night, that he had at his disposal methods of which I knew nothing. But between that and murder, assassination! No, no, a daughter cannot believe such things."

"So, on the Sunday, when Velmot came to fetch you at the Lodge while Noël Dorgeroux was out ... ?"

"That Sunday, he told me that my father had given up his plan and wanted to say good-bye to me and that he was waiting for me by the chapel in the disused cemetery, where the two of them had been experimenting with the fragments removed from the old wall in the Yard. As it happened, Velmot had taken advantage of his call at the Lodge to steal one of the blue phials which my uncle used. I did not notice this before he had already poured part of the liquid on the improvised screen of the chapel. I was able to get hold of the phial and throw it into the well. Just then you called me. Velmot made a rush at me and carried me to his motor-car, where, after stunning me with his fist and binding me, he hid me under a rug. When I recovered from my swoon, I was in the garage at Batignolles. It was in the evening. I was able to push the car under a window which opened on the street, and I jumped out. A gentleman and a lady who were passing picked me up, for I had sprained my ankle as I came to the ground. They took me home with them. Next morning I read in the papers that Noël Dorgeroux had been murdered."

Bérangère hid her face in her hands:

"Oh, how I suffered! Was I not responsible for his death? And I should have given myself up, if M. and Madame de Roncherolles, who were the kindest of friends to me, had not prevented me. To give myself up meant ruining my father and, as a consequence, destroying Noël Dorgeroux's secret. This last consideration decided me. I had to repair the wrong which I had unwittingly committed and to fight against those whom I had served. As soon as I was well again, I set to work. Knowing of the existence of the written instructions which Noël Dorgeroux had hidden behind the portrait of D'Alembert, I had myself driven to the Lodge on the evening before, or rather on the morning of the inauguration. My intention was to see you and tell you everything. But it so happened that the kitchen-entrance was open and that I was able to go upstairs without attracting anybody's attention. It was then that you surprised me, in god-father's bedroom."

"But why did you run away, Bérangère?"

"You had the documents; and that was enough."

"No, you ought to have stayed and explained."

"Then you shouldn't have spoken to me of love," she replied, sadly. "No one can love Massignac's daughter."

"And the result, my poor darling," I said, with a smile, "was that Massignac, who was in the house, of which he had a key, and who overheard our conversation, took the document and, through your fault, remained the sole possessor of the secret. Not to mention that you left me face to face with a formidable adversary!"

She shook her head: "You had nothing to fear from my father. Your danger came from Velmot; and him I watched."

"How?"

"I had accepted an invitation to stay at the Château de Pré-Bony, because I knew that my father and Velmot had lived in that neighbourhood during the past winter. Indeed, one day I recognized Velmot's car coming down the hill at Bougival. After some searching, I discovered the shed in which he kept his car. Well, on the fifteenth of May, I was watching there when he went in, accompanied by two men. From what they said I gathered that they had carried off my father at the end of the performance, that they had taken him to an island in the river where Velmot lay in hiding and that next day Velmot was to resort to every possible method to make him speak. I did not know what to do. To denounce Velmot to the police meant supplying them with convincing evidence against my father. On the other hand, my friends the Roncherolles were not at Pré-Bony. Longing for assistance, I ran to the Blue Lion and telephoned to you making an appointment with you there."

"I kept the appointment that same night, Bérangère."

"You came that night?" she asked, surprised.

"Of course I did; and at the door of the inn I was met by a small boy, sent by you, who took me to the island and to Velmot's house and to a room in which Velmot locked me up and from which, on the following day, I witnessed Théodore Massignac's torture and removal. My dear Bérangère, it wasn't very clever of you!"

She seemed stupefied and said: "I sent no boy. I never left the Blue Lion and I waited for you that night and all the morning. Somebody must have given us away: I can't think who."

"It's a simple enough mystery," I said, laughing. "Velmot no doubt had a crony of some sort in the inn, who told him of your telephone-call. Then he must have sent that boy, who was in his pay, to pick me up on my way to you."

"But why lay a trap for you and not for me?"

"Very likely he was waiting till next day to capture you. Very likely he was more afraid of me and wanted to seize the opportunity to keep me under lock and key until Massignac had spoken. Also no doubt he was obeying motives and yielding to necessities of which we shall never know and which moreover do not really matter. The fact remains, Bérangère, that, next day ..."

"Next day," she resumed, "I managed to find a boat and in the evening, to row round the island to the place where my father was dying. I was able to save him."

143

I in my turn was bewildered:

"What, it was you who saved him? You succeeded in landing, in finding Velmot in the dark, in hitting him just as he was turning on me? It was you who stopped him? It was you who set Massignac free?"

I took her little hand and kissed it with emotion. The dear girl! She also had done all she could to protect Noël Dorgeroux's secret; and with what courage, with what undaunted pluck, risking death twenty times over and not recoiling, at the great hour of danger, from the terrible act of taking life!

"You must tell me all this in detail, Bérangère. Go on with your story. Where did you take your father to?"

"To the river bank; and from there, in a market-gardener's cart, to the Château de Pré-Bony, where I nursed him."

"And Velmot?"

She gave a shudder:

"I did not see him again for days and days, not until this morning. I was sitting on the bench by the ruins, reading. Suddenly he stood before me. I tried to run away. He prevented me and said, 'Your father is dead. I have come to you from him. Listen!' I distrusted him but he went on to say, 'I swear I come from him; and, to prove it, he told me that you knew the formula. He confided it to you during his illness.' This was true. While I was nursing my father, in this very lodge, he said to me one day, 'I can't tell what may happen, Bérangère. It is possible that I shall destroy the screen at Meudon, out of revenge. It will be a mistake. In any case, I want to undo that act of madness beforehand.' He then made me learn the formula by heart. And this was a thing which no one except my father and myself could know, because I was alone with him and kept the secret. Velmot, consequently, was speaking the truth."

"What did you say?"

"I just said, 'Well?' Velmot said, 'His last wish was that you should give me the formula.' 'Never!' I said. 'You lie! My father made me swear never to reveal it to any one, whatever happened, except to one person.' He shrugged his shoulders: 'Victorien Beaugrand, I suppose?' 'Yes.' 'Victorien Beaugrand heard Massignac's last words. And he agrees with me, or at least is on the point of doing so.' 'I refuse to believe it!' 'Ask him for yourself. He's up there, in the ruins . . .'"

"I, in the ruins?"

"That's what he said: 'In the ruins, fastened to the foot of a tree. His life depends on you. I offer it to you in exchange for the formula. If not, he's a dead man.' I did not suspect the trap which he was laying for me. I ran towards the ruins as fast as I could. This was what Velmot wanted. The ruins was a deserted spot, which gave him the chance to attack me. He took it at once, without even trying to conceal his falsehood. 'Caught, baby!' he cried, throwing me to the ground. 'Oh, I knew you'd be sure to come! Only think, it's your lover, it's the man you love! For you do love him, don't you?' Evidently his only object was to obtain the secret from me by threats and blows. But what happened was that his rage against you and my hatred and loathing for him made him lose his head. First of all he wanted his revenge. He had me in his arms. Oh, the villain!"

She once more hid her face in her hands. She was very feverish; and I heard her stammering:

"The villain! ... I don't know how I got away from him. I was worn out. For all that, I managed to give him a savage bite and to release myself. He ran after me, brandishing his revolver; but just as he caught me up, he fell and let go of it. I picked it up at once. When he came after me again, I fired...."

She was silent. The painful story had exhausted her. Her face retained an expression of bewilderment and fright.

"My poor Bérangère," I said, "I have done you a great wrong. I have often, far too often, accused you in my heart, without guessing what a wonderful, plucky creature you were."

"You could not be expected to understand me."

"Why not?"

She murmured sadly:

"I am Massignac's daughter."

"No more of that!" I cried. "You are the one who always sacrificed herself and who always took the risk. And you are also the girl I love, Bérangère, the girl who gave me all her life and all her soul in a kiss. Remember Bérangère ... the other day in the Yard, when I found you again and when the sight of all those visions of love threw you in my arms...."

"I have forgotten nothing," she said, "and I never shall forget."

"Then you consent?"

Once again she repeated:

"I am Massignac's daughter."

"Is that the only reason why you refuse me?"

"Can you doubt it?"

I allowed a moment to pass and said:

"So that, if your fate had willed it that you were not Massignac's daughter, you would have consented to be my wife?"

"Yes," she said, gravely.

The hour had come to speak; and how happy was I to be able to do so. I repeated my sentence:

"If fate had willed that you were not Massignac's daughter....

Bérangère, did it never occur to you to wonder why there was so little affection between Massignac and you, why, on the contrary, there was so much indifference? When you were a child, the thought of going back to him and living with him used to upset you terribly. All your life was wrapped up in the Yard. All your love went out to Noël Dorgeroux. Don't you think, when all is said, that we are entitled to interpret your girlish feelings and instincts in a special sense?"

She looked at me in surprise:

"I don't understand," she said.

"You don't understand, because you have never thought about these things. For instance, is it natural that the death of the man whom you called your father should give you such an impression of deliverance and relief?"

She seemed dazed:

"Why do you say, the man whom I called my father?"

"Well," I replied, smiling, "I have never seen your birth-certificate. And, as I have no proof of a fact which seems to me improbable ..."

"But," she said, in a changed voice, "you have not the least proof either that it is not so...."

"Perhaps I have," I answered.

"Oh," said Bérangère, "it would be too terrible to say that and not to let me learn the truth at once!"

"Do you know Massignac's writing?"

I took a letter from my pocket and handed it to her:

"Read this, my darling. It is a letter which Massignac wrote to me and which he handed to me as he lay dying. I read only the first few words to begin with and at once went off in search of you. Read it, Bérangère, and have no doubts: it is the evidence of a dead man."

She took the letter and read aloud:

"Bérangère knows the formula and must not communicate it to any one except you alone, Victorien. You will marry her, will you not? She is not my daughter, but Noël Dorgeroux's. She was born five months after my marriage, as you can confirm by consulting the public records. Forgive me, both of you, and pray for me."

A long pause followed. Bérangère was weeping tears of joy. A radiant light was being thrown on her whole life. The awful weight that had bowed her down in shame and despair no longer bore upon her shoulders. She was at last able to breathe and hold her head high and look straight before her and accept her share of happiness and love. She whispered:

"Is it possible? Noël Dorgeroux's daughter? Is it possible?"

"It is possible," I said, "and it is certain. After his rightful struggle with Velmot and after the care which you bestowed upon him once you had saved him, Massignac repented. Thinking of the day of his death, he tried to atone for a part of his crimes and wrote you that letter ... which evidently possesses no legal value, but which you and I will accept as the truth. You are the daughter of Noël Dorgeroux, Bérangère, of the man whom you always loved as a father ... and who wanted us to be married. Will you dream of disobeying his wishes, Bérangère? Do you not think that it is our duty to join forces and together to complete his enterprise? You know the indispensable formula. By publishing it, we shall make Noël Dorgeroux's wonderful life-work endure for ever. Do you consent, Bérangère?"

She did not reply at once; and, when I again tried to convince her, I saw that she was listening with an absent expression, in which I was surprised to find a certain anxiety:

"What is it, darling? You accept, do you not?"

"Yes, yes," she said, "but, before everything I must try to jog my memory. Only think! How careless of me not to have written the formula down! Certainly, I know it by heart. But, all the same ..."

She thought for a long time, screwing up her forehead and moving her lips. Suddenly she said:

"A paper and pencil ... quickly...."

I handed her a writing-block. Swiftly, with a trembling hand, she jotted down a few figures. Then she stopped and looked at me with eyes full of anguish.

I understood the effort which she had made and, to calm her, said:

"Don't rack your brains now ... it'll come later.... What you need to-day is rest. Go to sleep, my darling."

"I must find it ... at all costs.... I must...."

"You'll find it some other time. You are tired now and excited. Rest yourself."

She did as I said and ended by falling asleep. But an hour after, she woke up, took the sheet of paper again and, in a moment or two, stammered:

"This is dreadful! My brain refuses to work! Oh, but it hurts, it hurts! ..."

The night was spent in these vain attempts. Her fever increased. Next day she was delirious and kept on muttering letters and figures which were never the same.

For a week, her life was despaired of. She suffered horribly with her head and wore herself out scribbling lines on her bed clothes.

When she became convalescent and had recovered her consciousness, we avoided the subject and did not refer to it for some time. But I felt that she never ceased to think of it and that she continued to seek the formula. At last, one day, she said with tears in her eyes:

"I have given up all hopes, dear. I repeated that formula a hundred times after I had learnt it; and I felt sure of my memory. But not a single recollection of it remains. It must have been when Velmot was clutching my throat. Everything grew dark, suddenly. I know now that I shall never remember."

She never did remember. The exhibitions at the Yard were not resumed. The miraculous visions did not reappear.

And yet what investigations were pursued! How many companies have been promoted which attempted to exploit the lost secret! But all in vain: the screen remained lifeless and empty, like a blind man's eyes.

To Bérangère and me it would have meant a sorrow incessantly renewed, if love had not brought us peace and consolation in all things. The authorities, who showed themselves fairly easy-going, I think, in this case, never found any traces of the woman who bore the name of Massignac. I was dispatched on a mission to the Far East. I sent out for her; and we were married without attracting attention.

We often speak of Noël Dorgeroux's great secret; and if Bérangère's lovely eyes become clouded with sadness:

"Certainly," I say, "the lost secret was a wonderful thing. There was never anything more thrilling than the Meudon pictures; and those which we had a right to expect might have opened up horizons which we are not able to conceive. But are you quite sure that we ought to regret them? Does a knowledge of the past and the future spell happiness for mankind? Is it not rather an essential law of our equilibrium that we should be obliged to live within the narrow confines of the present and to see before or behind us no more than lights which are still just glimmering and lights which are being faintly kindled? Our knowledge is adjusted to our strength; and it is not good to learn and to decipher too quickly truths to which we have not had time to adapt our existence and riddles which we do not yet deserve to know."

Benjamin Prévotelle made no attempt to conceal his disappointment. I keep up a regular correspondence with him. In every letter that I receive from this great scientist I anticipate his anxious question:

148

"Does she remember? May we hope?"

Alas, my answers leave him no illusions:

"Bérangère remembers nothing. You must not hope."

He consoles himself by waging a fierce contest with those who still deny any value to his theory; and it must be confessed that, now that the screen has been destroyed and it has become impossible to support that theory by proofs which are in any way material, the number of his adversaries has increased and that they propound objections which Benjamin Prévotelle must find it extremely difficult to refute. But he has every sincere and unprejudiced person on his side.

He likewise has the great public. We all know, of our reasoned conviction, and we all believe, out of our impulse of ardent faith, that, though we now receive no communications from our brothers in Venus, they, those beings with the Three Eyes, are still interesting themselves in us with the same fervour, the same watchfulness, the same impassioned curiosity. Looking down upon us, they follow our every action, they observe us, study us and pity us, they count our misfortunes and our wounds and perhaps also they envy us, when they witness our joys and when, in some secret place, they surprise a man and a maid, with love-laden eyes, whose lips unite in a kiss.

THE END

www.ingramcontent.com/pod-product-compliance
Lightning Source LLC
Chambersburg PA
CBHW020137180626
46810CB00004B/1606